DATE DUE

GAYLORD			PRINTED IN U.S.A.

British Library Cataloguing-in-Publication Data
A catalogue record for this book is available from the British Library

ISBN 0 86356 516 6
EAN 9 780863 565168

This edition first published 2005

SAQI

26 Westbourne Grove
London W2 5RH
www.saqibooks.com

Edwar al-Kharrat

STONES OF BOBELLO

Translated by Paul Starkey

SAQI

Bobello is an archaeological site containing Coptic tombs on a hill in the village of Tarrana (ancient Tarenthis) to the north of al-Khatatba in Beheira province. The main town in the area is Kafr Dawood.

It lies on a site that has been inhabited since prehistoric times. In ancient times it was a centre for caravan trade between the Nile Delta and the Libyan Desert. Around 600 ancient graves have been discovered there, with some 50 skeletons, all with wounds or gashes from axes or arrows.

In Graeco-Roman times it became a military garrison and a centre for the worship of the god Apollo (Bobello).

It is famous for its high quality Natron salts, and in Pharaonic times was a centre for the worship of Isis.

The lover knows not who his love might be
He has no destined lover.

Al-Imam al-Sha'rani, al-Anwar al-Qudsiya, *The Sacred Lights*

Contents

Preface

Edwar al-Kharrat was born in Alexandria in 1926 into a Coptic family and graduated in law from Alexandria University in 1946. From 1948 to 1950 he was detained for left-wing political activities and later worked for an insurance company. His first collection of short stories, *Hitan Aliya*, was published in 1958, but it was not until the emergence of the new group of writers usually known as the 'generation of the sixties' after the Arab-Israeli war of 1967, that he began to come to prominence, as editor of the literary magazine *Gallery 68*.

Al-Kharrat's is one of the most distinctive voices in contemporary Arabic literature. His first full-length novel, *Rama wa al-Tinnin*, published in 1979, was a landmark in modern Egyptian literary development and has often been hailed as the first expression of a 'new sensibility'. The work revolves around the relationship between the Copt Mikha'il and the Muslim Rama, a relationship that ranges between the mystical and the overtly sexual, and which constitutes a daring theme in view of the taboos on marriage between Muslim women and non-Muslim men. Many images from this work have reappeared in al-Kharrat's subsequent writing – not least, in the two semi-autobiographical works superbly translated into English by Frances Liardet under the titles *City of Saffron* (Quartet, 1989) and *Girls of Alexandria* (Quartet, 1993) respectively.

Readers of Frances Liardet's previously published translations will quickly find themselves at home in Stones of Bobello, which recounts a series of episodes from the author's childhood, most of them centred on the Egyptian Delta rather than the city environment of the previous two novels. As the author's own brief introductory note explains, Bobello itself is an archaeological site in the Delta province of Boheira, but though 'local colour' plays a large part in the work, it may also be read as a further expression of the age-old themes that haunt all al-Kharrat's writing – in particular, that of woman as a universal life force with neither beginning nor end. Though these themes are universal, at the same time al-Kharrat's language and technique is suffused in the Arabic literary tradition, and readers with knowledge of al-Kharrat's antecedents may well find echoes of themes from a previous age. For all the difference in geographical and cultural context, and for all the echoes of Proust remarked upon by previous commentators, I find it difficult to read the passage on pages 101–103 with its wanderings in the desert, its contrast between enduring rocks and fleeting humanity, and its memories of bygone love – without at the same time recalling the *qasidas* of the pre-Islamic poets.

***

Like much of al-Kharrat's work, *Bobello* is couched in language at once rich, subtle, and precise that poses formidable problems for any translator. In making the present version, I have been fortunate in having the support of the European Cultural Foundation in Amsterdam, whose Mémoires de la Méditerranné's project, started in 1994, aimed at bringing translations of modern Arabic autobiographical works to readers in a variety of European languages. As part of the process of translating *Bobello*, a group of translators gathered at the Toledo School of Translators in June 1999 to discuss our versions and to quiz the author on what lay behind the complexities of his original text. I am extremely grateful to Edwar al-Kharrat for the unstinting help that he provided, not only during that meeting, but also subsequently, when his comments and advice on my own draft translation proved invaluable.

Following the Toledo meeting, much of the final work of the translation was completed in Cairo during the summer of 2000. I am indebted to my family, Janet, Katie and Gavin, who patiently lived with the translation for much of this period; to the staff of the American University in Cairo Library for their help; to John Rodenbeck, for the loan of reference material; to Nina Prochazka, for her Maadi villa balcony; and to Maggie Kamel and Aziza Zaher, for advice on some particularly obtuse Egyptian colloquial expressions. I am also grateful to the French and Italian translators of *Bobello*, Jean-Pierre Milelli and Leonardo Capezzone respectively, whose already published translations provided occasional but valuable reference points when making the English version; the fact that I have disagreed with their interpretations on a number of occasions does not diminish my gratitude.

When this translation was originally commissioned, it was intended that it should be published (like those of Frances Liardet previously) by Quartet Books. Despite the great amount of work put in by the Quartet editor, Zelfa Hourani, this unfortunately proved impossible for financial reasons and, after a period of uncertainty, the project eventually had to be 'rescued' by Saqi Books. I remain grateful both to Zelfa for her constant support and optimism during the 'early days', and to Mai Ghoussoub and all the staff at Saqi Books for taking the project on, carrying it through to completion and ensuring that the translation has eventually seen the light of day.

Paul Starkey
Durham–Cairo, 1999–2004

1

The Ferry

You who abused our passion
Accepting the fire of separation
For you I sacrifice my soul

The old man's resonant voice was eloquent, solemn and moving.

We were in the ferry, a flat-bottomed, iron boat gliding gently and easily along the Beheira canal, and the smell of the water at the height of morning was pungent with the reek of vegetation.

On our way from Tarrana to the field to the west, behind 'Bobello', between the desert and the rich greenery of the other bank.

Apollo, the singer, the liberator, player of the lyre in ancient times – Apollo, who had now become the Beheira peasant Bobello, thanks to whom the waters had coursed in their murky channels for thousands of years carrying soil and silt, flood and flotsam – could this Apollo deliver me from plagues and reptiles, and from secret sins?

Could the light of the morning, at once beneficent and destructive, disperse what remained of the lingering night, shadows of suffering of a youthful body crushed by its never-ending desires?

With us in the ferry were my grandfather Sawiris, my maternal aunts Wadida and Sarah, Uncle Fanus who had almost died of love for Aunt Sarah but married Aunt Wadida, and the boy Barsum who was my own age.

Father Andrawus was also with us, and Uncle Gorgi, the blind church cantor, Khadra the peasant-woman, and Hamida, the leper.

But, above all, Linda and Rahma were with us, two graceful

houris, the joy and delight of the whole party, looking with admiration bordering on pure love at their father as he sang – his strong, tender voice quavering with the ripples of the water in the canal. I loved them both, Linda and Rahma together, and I was captivated by Khadra's charms and brazen femininity. In the midst of this triangle of women I found myself.

Uncle Selwanes was a land-tax collector, who covered an area in Menufiya and who slept in treasury rest-houses when he had finished collecting the taxes from the peasants and landowners. He would make his rounds on a splendid donkey of perfect beauty, attracting great respect, for his moral rectitude was untarnished by a single black spot, and his skill in writing and arithmetic was unsurpassed. He had an office in the tax department based in Shebin el-Kom. Now he was sad but relaxed, with both generosity and sorrow in his voice. He would pass through Tarrana from time to time, though I only occasionally saw him. His wife had died seven years ago and he had left the village as if he were punishing himself for some crime that he hadn't committed (or had he really committed it?) leaving his two daughters in the care of his sisters, Aunt Rosa and Aunt Salome, and of Khadra, who worked for them all, living with them and the buffaloes and the cows and the bull, keeping them all in order in the high, old house.

Strong-faced, with a dark yellow complexion, Uncle Selwanes's eyes were penetrating, sunk in their sockets, and green. His small hands, obviously skilled and strangely sensitive, seemed to be able to calm the raging of the water in the canal. His expensive, broadcloth galabiya was dark-coloured, almost the colour of water-moss, hanging down over the firm, muscular frame of his body as he sat calmly on the bench at the side of the boat singing, his heart full of emotion. He had a nephew studying at the Agricultural Institute in Shebin el-Kom – did Uncle Selwanes stay with them to sleep? – who would come to Tarrana in the summer vacation when we came from Alexandria, although he was some years older than me. The strange thing was that he was fair-haired, with a pale complexion, sturdy and tall, with a great presence and power of attraction. His galabiya was always white as snow, and his elastic ribbed shoes always black and shiny. I was jealous of him. It was understood and implicitly agreed that he would marry Rahma after he had taken his diploma.

From the ferry came the sound of the clanking of the chain that connected the two banks of the canal, as the ferryman pulled on it. Its links tautened, rattling in the background behind the crooning that was scarcely audible:

The nights have done their work on you
And long has been my moaning
The past came back to visit me
And left my heart lamenting

On the other side, the rusty iron chain was slack, its reddish links half-submerged in the water that churned with the silt of the circling flood, moving with the slow, gentle movement of the ferry as it passed across, carrying to us a sweet, watery breeze that invigorated our breasts, welcoming in the warmth of the first days of September.

We passed – we pass unceasingly – by the high, massive hill on the edge of the canal. The soft earth of centuries, the ruins of the divine temple, and the rough, trackless ground glistening with salt deposits. There was a matted mass of prickly esparto grass that hurt the eye, guarding the tombs of the Copts, the remnants of old passions of which nothing remained except harmless fragments of thick, green glass, shards of shiny pottery with inscriptions on them from omega to epsilon, and the howling of wolves defeated by the arrows of the bringer and conqueror of plagues, the protector and healer of mortals. Who will let me know your sacred or murderous desires? Uncle Selwanes, the heir who left no child, where is the chorus who will accompany you on your never-ending crossing?

I gaze at Rahma. I cannot take my eyes off her, despite her father's watchful gaze, and the stern look of my grandfather Sawiris, watching like a hawk ready to swoop, whose first and last blow to my face some weeks ago I have not forgotten and will never forget. He had caught me in the act of running after Linda in the alley, in the narrow cul-de-sac between our house and that of my uncle Arsanius, in the excitement of an improvised game of hind-and-seek at the height of noon. Half intentionally, I collided with her, and I felt, for a brief moment, her taut belly throbbing under my erection as she panted, then slipped from my arms with flushed face and knowing eyes, smiling as if despite herself. But it was Rahma that I was now staring at, enchanted. She was even smaller than me, and of slimmer build. Delicate, with a long face, light brown and drawn, no roundness of flesh in it but rather an easy smoothness. Had she drowned, this Rahma, in the waves of my dying, undying love, in the waves of the nights? This waxen, sculptured face, with its glazed look, which came to me in the salty waters of dreams, wasn't it the face of another woman, drowned in Lake Zurich? Or was it some woman who would drown in the future, whose drowning I did not yet know? I said: drowning is martyrdom. Or is it the face of a poet I loved who shot himself from love and died in vain? Who remembers him any more? She had slightly sunken eyes, she was slim and silent – unlike her younger sister who was soft-skinned, with a rounded bosom. She preferred to wear long, plain, dark-coloured clothes – unlike her sister who liked to wear flowery, coloured dresses, pleated at the hem – long, certainly, that went without saying, but a little wide at the bottom, which made them just a touch revealing.

The gloom of the fields became apparent to him, the hiding place of the hoopoes, the messengers of King Solomon, and of the ghosts. The waterwheels appeared to him, wrapped in shadows, crouching, like resting giants. The horizon echoed the groans of a waterwheel turning, as the water was raised, then fell back, and Egypt breathed, working by night as she worked by day, like a poet constantly fashioning an eternal poem from the quiet sorrows of his heart.

I asked my grandmother Amalia the story of Rahma and her cousin As'ad. 'Why do you ask, my child?' she said to me. 'Don't try to get between the onion and its skin ... Children nowadays! This girl's four years older than you. Like a snake in the grass, all's well on the surface, but disasters underneath!'

I avoid looking at Khadra, squatting beside Hamida the leper, on the damp iron floor of the ferry. It was naturally not right for her to sit on the wooden bench like her masters, how could it be right? Her arm was on the big basket, covered with a clean rag, well-washed but with faded colours – perhaps it was one of Linda's old dresses? Under her almost transparent black galabiya could be seen another galabiya, decorated with lots of little red flowers. Was this also one of Linda's dresses? Her thin, black veil hung down over her back to the floor of the ferry. With her hand clutching the edge of her veil she hid half her dark, pretty face. Her round, bent thighs were a little raised, as she squatted beneath us on the slightly damp floor.

She drew in her legs and folded them under her. Her thighs appeared even rounder and peculiarly soft, even under the galabiyas which she had wrapped firmly and carefully around them, in a way that betrayed no conscious intention to arouse, but which was, for this very reason, extremely arousing. I didn't want to look at her, but I couldn't forget her.

Here I am, crossing from one bank to the other, constantly, with no beginning and no end, a large, red, bronze one-millime piece on my mouth, holding it shut, the ferryman's fare.

The ferryman was dumb, with a coarse face, and eyes that never shut. He had a secret hideaway on the far bank.

Tirelessly I pursue the killer of the dragon, carrying for him an atonement for his sin, exiled in the icy land in the north, the most distant reach of civilisation, and with him, despite all the women of lust and drunkenness and desire, I seek order and reason, justice and music.

I shall never arrive, I shall never pay the fare, always between two banks.

I know this. How could I not know it?

Inside this triangle of women the song shook my fresh, gullible heart.

***

In Tarrana, in my grandmother Amalia's house, I had made some bright red ink with my own hands, from some finely powdered clothes dye I had found.

On almost transparent paper, slightly grey (paper was expensive and difficult to obtain in the second year of the war and I still hoard white lined paper like a starving man hoarding loaves of bread that he will never eat) and with a black wooden pen with a fine bronze nib, in schoolboy language, I would write on the table, squatting on a cushion.

Just before we left Tarrana, as we got ready to ride the donkeys to the ferry point on the canal, the postman, Eryan Effendi, arrived in the small yard in front of my grandfather Sawiris's house, under the enormous sycamore tree. Under his tarboosh was a handkerchief with pale blue squares, slightly dirty and damp with sweat around the edges. Energetic and hearty, though slim enough to pass through the eye of a needle, he would clap his hands before he had finished dismounting from his tall, white, official donkey, and shout, 'Uncle Sawiris! Post! Good morning, everyone, good and generous people! Khadra, my girl, come on, give me a drop of water! I'm dying of thirst, girl!' And he would look at her with a look of unadulterated desire, as he handed her the post.

There was nothing in the post except *al-Ahram*, to which we subscribed and which came to us every day by express train, arriving at Kafr Dawood station and the post office at exactly eight o'clock in the morning, and *al-Ithnayn wa al-Dunya*[1] magazine, a copy of which reached us once in a blue moon, sent by my father from Alexandria when he could.

Among many other fascinating things that I knew nothing about, my attention was caught by the fact that the queen of the music-hall revue, Badi'a Masabni, would be at the Opera Casino in Ibrahim Square (tel: 44814) from Saturday 30 November 1940 presenting a second musical revue, *Two Lucky Hours* – seven scenes packed with novelties and surprises by the famous maestro Abu al-Sa'ud al-Ibyari, set to music by the composer Farid Ghusn, with dance *mis-en-scene* by 'Professor' Isaac Dixon, and the participation of world-famous dancer Tahiyya Carioca and popular comic actor Isma'il Yasin, with first-class restaurant, American bar and music-hall.

In the dust of Tarrana, with its coarse and artless greenery, that was really tempting. I didn't know exactly what a music-hall was.

Why then did I imagine it as a spacious, almost deserted courtyard, tiled with polished flagstones, with a great, wide piano in it on a great, high dais, and dancing girls like those in the magazines whose pictures had excited me – I hadn't yet seen them in the cinema – like the girl who aroused me as I fantasised about her body, and through whom the first pleasures of sexual awareness had come upon me as I experienced an innocent, almost childish ejaculation, in number 211 of that same Ithnayn magazine, shortly (two years, maybe?) before the war? Her name was Su'ad Fahmi, and she was with the Beba troupe at the Monte Carlo Casino. Despite being a native of Alexandria, however, I knew nothing about this Casino yet, except for the sign on the Corniche when I passed it, with my hand in my mother's, on our way to the ladies' bath at Chatby on Wednesdays.

The fire turned in his languid eyes, the words shivered on his dry lips, but he cast no glance at her. He walked slowly, then threw aside the curtain from the window of his balcony that the sagging branches of the vine embraced like a grief-stricken mother clutching her beloved daughter to her heart, fragrant with the breath of the white blossom and aflame with the warm, heavy perfume that fell from the giant mulberry tree, like the warmth flooding through a tomb where candles were burning.

Su'ad Fahmi was wearing a dress with a wide slash under the armpits, through which could be seen a part of her pert breast. The opening extended to the middle of her waist. The fabric of the dress followed her curves, clinging to her belly, waist and thighs as it fell down to her legs, split at the side, reaching the floor in folds like waves. A twisted sash of shiny cloth encircled her waist. She was clasping the edge of the sash tightly and firmly over the top of her belly, holding it with her thumb while she spread her hand over her belly, her nails painted with dark shadow. The bromide technique used by Dar al-Hilal had produced a picture somewhere between dull grey and the colour of ash, with just a hint of pale blue in it. She was raising her naked arm over her small breasts, and her eyes had a reckless look of seduction in them; her thick, dark, heavy hair hung over her narrow brow in a luxuriantly formed half circle, falling to her bare shoulders.

I never made love, in fact, except with fantasy bodies. Even at their most bodily and earthly, they were still fantasies.

As for the thunderbolts of love and sex to which I fell prey (so to speak), they struck me three times. I could not ward them off; the scales shuddered with the deadly charge, and the monstrous serpent's armour rattled to no avail.

I had been to Cairo only once that I can recall, some years ago when I was very young. We were visiting the agricultural and industrial exhibition (possibly eight years previously, in 1932?) and we went to the house of a relative of ours, a tram conductor, beside the railway line, in rain that had turned the narrow alley into an impossibly muddy passageway. We spent the night with my aunt Dimaris in Shubra, and I woke at dawn the next morning to the sound of the call to prayer, sweeter and more plaintive than I have ever heard it before or since. It resounded in the tranquil stillness of the dawn, to be followed by an indescribable peace, the beauty of its reverberations never ceasing. The call of the muezzin that day to 'come to prayer', the two confessions of belief chanted with such deep faith, had an enduring resonance that has never left the chambers of my soul with its inexhaustible and insatiable desires.

Ah! ...

From the balcony he could see the warm, dark earth of an Egypt that had cloaked itself in a transparent nightgown.

He saw the stars twinkling like small fires burning in the blue sky, their glow reflected in the waters of the Nile which flowed on majestically, humming ancient tunes in a harmonious blend of melodies and languages, while on her banks the water nymphs stretched out in the summer's night, cloaking themselves in the light of the stars, whispering tales of myths and fables that are ever new and never die. Dreaded maidens of the night, slumbering on the shore in their everlasting night, with their black, unkempt hair, and their deep, tranquil eyes that entice anyone fate leads into their arms, to fling himself onto their soft bosoms – only to plunge to the depths with him and emerge alone with bloody lips, their eyes gleaming with an icy fire.

In the morning, after a breakfast of homemade *ful mudammis* with butter, fresh *bettour* bread, and tea with milk in a lightly coloured green glass, I would almost every day, sometimes twice a day, visit Rahma and Linda's house, that is Aunt Salome and Aunt Rosa's house.

Their house was one of the few houses in Tarrana of two storeys, at the end of a narrow, twisting lane that ended suddenly in a dead-end, with a wall. The soft mud stuck to my bare feet exposed in their backless slippers, for who would bother to wear proper shoes in the village, on a morning? Hadn't schooldays finished, and with them the need to bother about one's appearance? A galabiya or striped pyjamas were all one needed. I was careful not to let my feet sink into the fresh, round balls of dung, knowing that Khadra would be collecting them to make the lumps of dry fuel that I could see lined up on the roof of the house.

The entrance to the house lay between the surround of the cattle-pen and the blank end-wall built of sun-dried mud brick. It was roofed, narrow and dark, set behind an ancient wooden door, with a latch (also of wood) raised by a rope pulled from the upper floor above to open it. (The latch would then fall back into a slot made on the inside of the door.) The animals had been gone from the shelter of the pen since early morning, but their smell was still thick and heavy, stifling the senses, ever present.

When I went in, Khadra was sweeping the pen with a rough, palm-leaf broom, held together with a stripped acacia branch, its knots still visible.

In a stained and faded black work galabiya, with a vertical slit at the side that reached to below her waist, through which could be seen a dingy, coarsely woven, pale green undershirt, and through which her dark, youthful breast was slipping, quivering, firm but tender, and extraordinarily arousing, under her dirty clothes, she worked without paying the slightest attention to my hungry but bashful look.

Her little daughter was playing with a dry corn cob, half of which had been stripped of the dry corn. She had wrapped her head in a dark cloth, under which one could see her matted blonde hair. She looked at me with wide, green, wondering eyes, which seemed to be flirting unashamedly.

Her youngest child was clinging to his mother's legs as she swept, swaying as he pulled at her galabiya, with nothing on him but a short shirt that showed his little penis, his innocent testicles, and his slightly bowed legs.

'Go inside, child, go on with you ... put some clothes on him, my girl ... shame on you!'

But he looked at me cheekily, the cheek of a new child's life that has sprung from the warmth of the dung, the huge mass of the buffalo, and the yearning of the earth that, almost unconsciously and without hesitation, challenges the constraints and confinements of walls.

The other girls were wandering about in the courtyard under the palm tree or in front of the house in the open space hidden from the road. Did I see in the corner of the pen the shadows of

21

several men? Or did I see a single man, looking like many? Was it the fair-haired As'ad, or Uncle Selwanes with his green, piercing eyes that lit up the shadows of the bower? Was it Khadra's husband Hegazi, or the shadow of the effendi from Alexandria, son of Uncle Qaldas from Upper Egypt – who came from Ragheb Pasha and who was dying of love for the two houris Linda and Rahma, burning with the fires of unquenchable desire? Did men's shadows always lie in wait for me and my women? No, but he was there, I saw him in the morning gloom.

I knew that Hegazi, the hired labourer, worked one day and was idle for several. He travelled for months with the itinerant labourers in the work season, but Khadra still got pregnant every year.

When he was staying in the village, he would sometimes take the animals to pasture by the irrigation channels, or the main canal, or the embankment by the big river.

That was a job for the young boys – or even the young girls – but poverty is a harsh beast. The man had the face of a beast and a victim at the same time, rough, pock-marked and dry, like the branch of an old sycamore tree, but with the tree's latent vigour also. I saw him sweep out the pen once, clearing from it the old, encrusted layers of animal droppings, which he would roll together with the fresh dung, then fashion into flat disks, just as the women did, and spread them out in the courtyard under the palm-tree to make fuel. He was wearing a piece of sacking, matted with dirt, over his skin.

He and Khadra, with her latest child and the five girls, would all sleep with the animals in a corner of the pen – whether to guard them, or just for the company, I don't know, but they seemed to enjoy it, anyway!

'Good day, Khadra!'

'Good day to you, sir, and may God keep your every step secure!'

He lifted his face to the heavens and saw the fragile, eternal stars encircling a small, pale moon that was clothed in a transparent, white cloud.

The stars were the ruins of a white castle whose remains had been dispersed and debris scattered around a semi-circular lake of tranquil silver. He saw the beautiful clouds silently wafting towards an unknown, magical earth, dreamlike sails transporting in their vessels the sons of gods as they slept, the sons of Khonso Apollo and his daughters, lunar suns.

His flushed face was brushed by the breezes of a warm wind, fragrant on its edges with the scent of wild flowers that wafted from the graveyard where trees shaded the ghosts of the graves, where crumbling bones sighed under the barren palms and acacia trees, where the roots of the Christ's-thorn and sycamores struck into the ground through the dark eyes of skulls that stared without blinking in their eternal night, and where the trunks of the mulberry and mango trees pierced through the skeletons in the ground, bearing their succulent leaves, shining and open, into the light of the sky.

'Aunt Rosa, Aunt Salome,' I called from below.

Neither of them was really my aunt, they were more like aunts to my mother. Their cousin was Hanna Bey who lived in a side street off Rassafa in Alexandria. My mother liked to give him a share of the special Angel Mikhail pie that she made for me on his feast day. He had a son with the same name as me, but considerably older than me – quite ancient, in fact. He was a traditional poet, rather mediocre, but he had nevertheless acquired a certain reputation.

I heard the high, cracked voice:

'Come on up, child, come on, my dear! Linda, Rahma! See to your cousin, open the cool reception room!'

Aunt Rosa and Aunt Salome were twins, fashioned in a single mould. I never ever saw them – even at the height of summer – in anything except a long, black dress with an ornament made of shiny silk material on the breast, and a high closed collar firmly encircling the scrawny, wrinkled neck, like the neck of an old turkey cock! In summer, they wore mens' black shoes with flat heels, and in winter, high-heeled boots with round leather buttons in a row up their thin legs, with thick socks in summer and winter alike. When it turned cold at the end of September, I saw them visiting Grandmother Amalia with an old-fashioned black silk overcoat over their dresses.

Not a hint of breast or bottom could be seen on them. They were completely flat, and stood bolt upright, dry and emaciated.

Their stinginess was proverbial in the whole of Tarrana, and with good reason.

'Watch out, or you'll be like Rosa. I've never even got a cup of tea out of her!'

'Like Salome, a dried up corn-cob ... not a drop of water in her!'

People used to talk about a treasure-trove of gold coins, Ottoman and English, and big bank-notes like green handkerchiefs, with pictures of minarets on them[2] – a cache hidden away in a hole covered with sunbaked mud bricks under the iron bed with the high legs, some said – or else it was in the clay *mastaba* upstairs, in the other reception room that was never opened for anyone, under piles of cotton mattresses and blankets and carpets from Asyut, or under the south-facing window that was always shut – the window with the wide ledge where they had put the books of chants, Coptic language teaching books, the *Thousand* and *One Nights* in four parts, with its covers missing, and one part of a lithographed version of the *Aghani*[3] on yellowed, dried-up paper, so fragile that it was on the point of disintegrating.

The door was never opened after the evening call to prayer that came from the distance, from the mosque that looked out over the Beheira canal.

Khadra, Hegazi (when he was in town) and their children would sleep from the time of the evening prayer until the morning star appeared. The aunts were like watchmen, like two kites waiting to swoop.

Linda and Rahma used to sleep at our house, that is at my grandfather Sawiris's house, if they had decided to spend the evening or eat supper with us. They had first to secure the necessary permission, of course, especially in those days, when Aunt Wadida was engaged to Uncle Fanus, and all the girls and women of the family, and our female relatives and neighbours, would form groups to sing peasant songs and improvise on the rustic drums, on the open *mastaba* of our house, by the light of red flames dancing in the lamps made from tin cans that we called 'Sheikh Alis'.

What stubborn insistence was it that drove me, in the midst of the idealism of shy, repressed love and the upsets of the heart, the frustrations of peasant customs and relentless tradition, and the storms of secret passion – what insistence was it that drove me by the fragile, flickering light of 'Sheikh Ali' to continue writing in light red ink, as I sat on the hard mattress, resting the flimsy, half-grey paper on a bed of old pages from *al-Ahram* spread out on the wood of the low table?

A shudder went through his body.

He was in the Egyptian countryside, in the cavern of his dreams, in the abode of his gods, the land of magic, fable and phantoms, the cradle of hardship and labour, where life was always on the brink of death.

He left the warm breeze wafting from the open balcony, and leaned his back against the wall, gazing at his temple.

In silent devotion.

He said, 'Isn't that simple, suffering youth still there in one of the corners of your soul? Are you still protecting him, even?'

'Wouldn't you like him to die, with his naive poetry that is worth, in the poetry market, not a farthing? Wouldn't you like him to pass away?'

He said, 'Could he have been embalmed already? Behind a mask that is open for all to see? Could his skull have been wrapped in a shroud of torn linen, with only a few glass crystals (sparkling or faded) remaining? Salt crystals from Natrun?'

He said, 'No, alive and well, like it or not, it's all the same.'

He said, 'Buried beneath the dust of words.'

2
Bobello

We reached the western field and disembarked from the ferry onto the wooden gangplank that the ferryman had extended to the bank of the canal, over black damp earth oozing with moisture from the flood water hidden in the rich substance of the soil. The sun was already hot.

Under a circle formed of acacia trees, gazorina, and a single Christ's thorn with an enormous trunk – an ancient tree with sagging branches – we spread fresh green corn leaves on the ground, one layer on the other.

Khadra was fanning the flames of the fire that had been kindled from cotton stalks and corn cobs.

The corn cobs, stripped just a moment ago of their green, silky wrappings, crackled on the quickly dying embers that Khadra was still feeding with tinder, fanning it with the side of a flat rusty piece of metal which still bore traces of the drawing of a shell and, in faded red, the word 'Shell'. Smoke rose from an improvised cooker made of two bricks standing on end. The rising rings of smoke carried a piercing heat from the fire, but the wisps soon dispersed, disappearing into the air.

We lunched on round, layered pastries, dripping with clarified butter, with which I was given a fried duck's leg, sweet and rich – the richness of ducks fattened by my grandmother Amalia as she held them under her legs, stuffing them twice a day with beans, corn and pellets made with bran, meal and a little sesame, and kneaded with water.

My grandfather Sawiris invited me to take some reddish-brown cognac in a small tumbler of ribbed glass that gleamed and glistened under the delicate shimmering of the shadows and the light of the sun.

The wind had got up as late afternoon approached. The trees rustled musically, and the reddish flood water that was pouring into the canal grumbled and gurgled quietly as the waves and eddies met each other. We brushed off the flies that had collected around us and which landed on us constantly, without respite. The reed fly-whisk with its slender twirls and ivory handle made a sort of whistling, scraping noise in the hands of Uncle Selwanes and Grandfather Sawiris that made the skin prickle. The buzzing of the wasps, the fluttering of the butterflies with their swift, transparent, silver wings, and the lowing of the buffalo tethered to the waterwheel – all these mingled in my ears, sharpened and sensitised by the cognac, with Uncle Selwanes's humming and his hidden sadness – *Accepting the fire of separation, You who kept affection, I heard the whisper of the heart, I give my soul for you* – and the inevitable barking of the dog that rang out insistently, fearfully from the edges of the fields.

As the day drew to a close, I went to the end of the circle spread with the now tatty corn leaves. The rays of the setting sun came to us from the side, soft and spreading, shadowless. I tucked my bare legs under my white galabiya, its edges now dirty, and sat beside Khadra, beside her round thigh, as she squatted at a respectful distance from the 'gentlemen'. She knew her place, but she was still almost regal – the proud possessor of a luxurious body that brimmed over with a wealth of worldly wisdom, innocence and unspoken knowledge at the same time.

'Khadra', I said to her, 'strip another corn cob for me. Please!!'

She looked at the little child that was me with a look of conspiracy and complicity, the boldness of a woman teaching a young boy how to recognise his masculinity.

I ate the fresh corn cob raw, my mouth dripping with the milky liquid that had a light and surprising sweetness, while large ants, thieves of the cooking pots, light brown in colour, ran at lightning speed from between my legs and under her thighs, carrying their food from the broad green corn leaves, fleeing with it into their holes, the entrances to which were clearly visible in the canal bank.

'Bobello? The Hill of the Cursed?' said Khadra, in a disinterested way. 'See how our Lord's anger brought them down and destroyed them! I take refuge in God from the anger of God!'

* * *

My awareness of the soft, relaxed, brown flesh was keen now, keen and tense. The pleasure of the sensation was repeated, vivid and undimmed.

Is it a recollection that keeps returning? Is it now the violent effect of the cognac, of the rich greasy food, and the sweetness of the earth's rich fruits? Or is it the excitement of the headstrong imaginings of youth?

Had she taught me lust, in all its different forms?

Or was this torment a disturbance of the gods?

The smell of the damp earth drying in the heat of the day, the odour of the green corn leaves dying under us and the occasional whiff of buffalo dung all seemed to increase the frenzy of the earthy intoxication hidden in my soul.

Khadra had covered her head with a thin black veil that slipped down a little over her shoulders, revealing a blue circle, a dark, slightly uncertain blue, under the black weave of the veil that shimmered in the light. Her luxuriant hair fell in two plaits over her back, wound round with a headband of blue cloth, that seemed now to shine as it encircled her jet black hair.

I heard Aunt Rosa asking Khadra to rub her hair with paraffin, a request she made regularly, at the start of every month, to get rid of all the parasites.

After the paraffin had dried, spreading its aroma through the entrance of the house, I saw Khadra rub it in slowly, with a sensual movement.

She shut on herself the wooden door that closed the mud-walled hut in the animal pen and darkened it.

From above, as I read Aunt Rosa some pages of the Thousand and One Nights, I could hear the hiss of the paraffin lamp under the water can that was filled at the stone jetty in the Nile, where the waters ran faster and clearer. When I went down, I smelled on her the fragrance of the Quassis eau de cologne that I had bought from the Tuesday market in Kafr Dawood and secretly given to Khadra as a present.

The waves of her black hair flowed over my side and breast and the top of my abdomen as she bent over me secretly in the darkness. Outside, the day was bright with the morning sun. Her hair had a strange, pungent smell. She told me once that she used to grind cloves in a mortar with incense and dried pomegranate peel, soaking the powder in a little olive oil with some alcohol and a spot of sandalwood perfume, extracting from it a substance to rub into her hair. She said, 'You could make my hair smell like a lioness in heat!' The feel of her moist lips as they closed around me, their warmth, their teasing touch! The pleasure of it was indescribable. When I was about to reach a climax (who can bear the agony of ecstasy and the approach of fulfilment?), then, with a practised, carnal intelligence she would lift her mouth to prolong the moment.

I was driven crazy by her sensuality.

She seized me and carried me off in the violent spasms of her body, a desert from which there was no escape, no escape even until now.

I have hidden your body in my heart, throbbing, demanding, tempestuously alive, to this day, to this day...

He said that the oriental lamps decorated with brass poured out a gentle blue light, throwing soft, quivering rays and faint shadows here and there. Between the patches of brightness and the gloom of the shadows small statues were scattered, captivating and dreamlike, the remains of a soul frozen in fragments carved from life.

His eyes settled only on his last statue.

He had poured into the soft, white marble every cup of a life filled with the wine of sorrows and dreams, the wine of ecstasy and sorrow, the drunkenness of a heart that takes no account.

He looked at her amazed. His soul is her holy of holies, an altar for her incense, her protective fortress. Under her feet were scattered splinters of rocks, fragments of marble with shining edges, and his strong iron tools – chisels, knives, hooks, needles and drills. She was living, she, among the remains of the sculpture, the fantasies of the shadows and the trembling yearning of the light.

He ran his fevered hands through his dusty, matted hair.

A girl, a houri, a goddess, from Egypt, are you dreaming?

Or do you see what mortals cannot see? Reclining in her marble bedchamber with flowing folds, her soft body draped in a folded, loosely hanging gown that seemed to embrace her soul, passionately. She raised her thin, smooth, marble face, supporting her elegant head on naked arms of ivory, her hair loose, bright tresses of stone, eyes deep in their sockets, hinting at a boundless expanse, with a hidden, inner light. She had let her heavy lids fall over her eyes, her lashes casting long shadows over her smooth, pale cheek, with its soft, sharply rounded edges, and her full lips were half open, ready to submit.

Silent, her sighing unspoken, in an obscure, unseen, incandescence.

* * *

Even before we arrived at the western field, Bobello rose to an impressive height. The hills from which the fellahin carried off basketfuls of the rich, camphorous manure were divided in almost vertical lines by hoe marks.

A pile of potsherds, thick pieces of glass coloured Pharaonic blue or a translucent dark yellow, soft in the hands and no longer sharp, gypsum and sandstone with half-erased inscriptions in hieroglyphs, demotic, Greek and Kufic Arabic script. The long succession of years had heaped up barren piles of stones and glass and marble debris. The years had seen them buried under heaps of earth, in which one could see gaping holes where generations of patient, persistent hands, grandfather to father, had scooped hollows in the fertile manure. The remains of dead bodies and the fragments of souls that could find no rest save in the earth of fields irrigated with flood water and silt. The dust of priests, people, soldiers and merchants feeds the wheat, clover and barley, mingling with the sap of the roots of the endless succession of sycamores and the venerable Christ's thorn. The soft stalks of corn with their sugary grains – a chain with shining links or a revenge that the eternal peasant is taking for us and for himself? Does he die now amid the flickerings of the video and the electrification of cement and bricks? Son of light, enemy of darkness and of all its dried up offspring, does he still strike the earth with his hoe – does he still? – just as he makes love to his wife, and receives the first basket loads of the harvests that he has ripened, watering them with the ancient honey of the Nile, protecting them from the scorching heat of summer where the floodwaters do not reach, and from the excreta of insects and worms, the gnawing of rats and the ravages of locusts?

* * *

In the afternoon, practically every day, I would go to the house of my uncle Arsanius and his son Fanus (who would marry Aunt Wadida), to find Rahma.

To meet her.

We would go out together from there, to stroll around.

I would comb my thick hair with Brilliantine and change my daytime galabiya, putting on another that was clean as snow. I would wipe my open sandals in which I would later come back dirty, mud sticking to the soles from the splashes on the Nile embankment. We would wander around the wide threshing floor where the flood water was beginning to seep, slowly at first, gradually rising until it became a wide pool in which the sparkle of the stagnant water hid little fish that the peasant children caught in tin mugs, or else grabbed quickly and cleverly in their hands. Where had the fish come from? This European-style promenade did not occasion anyone's surprise at that time, though I can imagine the likely (indeed, the actual) reaction now from mischievous village children and their families, from the men with beards and short galabiyas (who didn't exist at that time), and from people obsessed with the idea that women are an obscenity to be kept under wraps. In those days people knew that there was a time for the heart and a time for the Lord.

Rahma and I would go as far as the big deserted waterwheel, under the raised embankment by the Nile. We climbed down to it on stones wedged into the side of the earth embankment, which was crumbly on top, but firm and solid by the broad bank. We almost slipped, laughing from fear of falling. I would cling on to her hand with its delicate, almost transparent, bones, feeling it tremble from an ecstasy of the senses, affection and an inexplicable veneration. We would sit on the wide open space by the shore, close to the swirling water, on the cracked and dirty wooden arm, black and bent now from the drought, that hung from the massive water-wheel slightly sunk in the earth of the bank. Year after year at the height of the flood, the waters would rise so far as to submerge the underside of this massive arm, leaving on it, after they had subsided, a slightly wavy line and marking it with a dingy colour that stayed dark until the following year.

Rahma did not talk much, unlike her sister Linda who enjoyed prattling on in her ungrammatical, peasant Arabic with its delightful sounds and rhythm. Sometimes, though, she would ask me about my lessons in the 'Abbasiyya secondary school ('What do you learn there?') and about the news of the war in the newspapers, and I would give her a learned and eloquent account, with a spontaneity that I later rarely knew with women.

I told her that in the middle of Europe (the land of the Franks, in other words), there was a region called Bohemia inhabited by people called Czechs and others called Slovaks, for which reason it had the difficult name of Czechoslovakia that nobody in Tarrana could pronounce properly or easily except for Aunt Wadida. It had now fallen into Hitler's hands – Hitler being well known in Tarrana – and the British and French allies had to re-examine the problem of Bohemia's independence in order to avoid another war. The Czech people had a centuries-old history of civilisation, and there were now dreams, and plans, to appoint a king who would rule Bohemia, Slovakia and Hungary at the same time, with three thrones in three capitals, Prague, Bratislava and Budapest. I told her that British planes had dropped leaflets on Hamburg and Berlin calling on the Germans to surrender, and I also told her about Lady Elizabeth Pearce, the sister of the Duke of Northumberland, whose engagement had been announced to the Marquis of Douglas – the engagement representing a happy end to a long-running feud between the couple's families that had lasted for some six hundred years. On the same theme, I also told her about Romeo and Juliet and their dreadful fate, and her eyes became a little moist. I pronounced the names crisply, with an authentic English accent, but she paid no attention to that. She was simply fascinated by the tale of love, listening to me intently, with her deep, honey-coloured eyes fixed on me, as if she had left her body behind as the sun set. The crows' cawing grew louder and more persistent on the acacia and mulberry trees above, while from up on the high embankment that seemed far away and cut off from us, came the lowing of the cattle and buffaloes, and the bleating of sheep returning from the fields. We would have to climb up and go back before twilight descended, or else we would be in trouble with our family – and what trouble!

With her gentle breaths and dreamy sighs, he imagined that her spirit was relaxing. Her small breasts seemed to be trembling over an anxious beating heart, in the throes of a dream overcome by melancholy. Her veil was thrown over her outstretched legs as if trying to kiss her feet (as he too longed to). Then she dozed off, tired and exhausted, in a flood of faraway dreams, while from the fragments of her soul there shone with unseen radiance a sad humility like the night-time of life. Who was she? A goddess, or a disembodied ghost, a fantasy given substance by the marble and the light? She looked at him, saying, 'Come. Come to me, my weary one! Come to my arms, find rest in my bosom!' Was she a dream, a figment of the imagination of a fickle youth in love? Or was she, despite her inert substance, throbbing with life, real life? He went towards her like a man bewitched, shut his eyes, approached and bowed.

'Now I know how the Egyptians worshipped their goddesses,' he said, 'and how their goddesses were immortal and undying.'

'A goddess?' he said. 'A thing? A woman? Or is it simply she?'

Her eyelids were still lowered as she looked at him from behind her lashes, dreaming her gentle or malicious dreams. She had nothing to do with him, she was free, separate. She was not his thing, she was not his.

***

On the way to Bobello we passed our graveyards on dusty unmarked footpaths beside earth oozing with salt water, crusty and silvery in the sun.

We climbed up to the small hill, scattered with tombs with small, half-collapsed domes, old tombs fallen to the ground, and piles of small stones and rubble. Whose tombs they were, nobody could remember any longer. Many years later, my mother would instruct me to bury her (only after a long life, I said to her!) beside her father, my grandfather Sawiris, in Bobello. She repeated the instruction insistently and I promised her faithfully, but I could not keep the promise. I had an expensive tomb made for her in the Chatby1 cemetery, at the end of some forlorn street, and I do not know, or care, if I will be buried there beside her, or if my children will have to be content with an improvised grave in the cemeteries of Mar Gorgis in Old Cairo.

We turned off towards the small, locked church, which the priest opened with his large, iron key. Uncle Gorgi felt his way across the ground with his thick stick, surely and confidently, and made his way straight to the sanctuary, striking the floor covered with ancient marble. Uncle Gorgi, the church cantor, could light a cigarette with a magnifying glass from the light of the sun, with nothing more than the touch of his practised fingers. We stood behind Father Andrawus and he recited a short prayer for us, without opening the altar area, or even going through the screen to enter the sanctuary. Then we recited the Lord's Prayer and I mumbled it with them, though I had never learned it by heart and still have not done so. We knelt in front of the screen, made the sign of the cross and the priest blessed us and gave us absolution. Then we went out into the blinding light of the morning sun and put offerings on the tombs of ancestors and forebears whom I scarcely knew. The tomb's dwelling is an eternal exile from which there is no escape, it is the final homeland. Where, though, have the peasant children come from, jumping about like goats with their faded, patched galabiyas over their bodies, and hair ruffled under dusty, spattered skullcaps? (May God have mercy on your dead, Khawaga Arsani, may God have mercy on your dead, Mu'allim Fanus.) Linda, Rahma and Khadra gave them portions of biscuits, warm bettour bread baked at dawn, and dried dates.

We stayed together for the rest of the day, our limbs filled with pure, sensual, physical pleasure. How can one describe the fullness of that ecstasy that permeates to the core of the body, whatever has been said about it over the years?

In the afternoon, on the bank of the canal, the girls and women would wash clothes and dishes, brass cooking pots, earthenware pots and tin plates. Their galabiyas were deliberately pulled up to reveal their brown thighs, in full view of everyone, as if there were was not the slightest reason to be embarrassed. They rubbed, wrung and rinsed energetically, laughing and chattering as if they were enjoying a moment of rest from their toil, rather than a period of hard labour that consumed all their energies.

The animals were returning from the fields in a long line, kicking up the soft earth which wrapped them in a cloud and left a rough taste in my mouth – like a copy of an ancient sculpture that had acquired flesh and movement, a picture that I never weary of recalling from thousands of years ago, contemporary yet timeless. A buffalo with protruding bones stopped as we walked down the gangplank extended over the edge of the embankment to take the ferry – a beast from prehistoric times, from before time itself, faded black in colour. Suddenly it lifted its tail, and in front of us we could see the exposed, rectangular slit with its pale pink flesh, soft, firm and quivering, from which rippled forth a fountain of water, clean and clear, astonishingly clean, in fact, as it gushed out without the slightest embarrassment.

I remembered the stories about the boy Barsum and his sexual adventures with buffaloes.

And I thought – a little simple-mindedly – wasn't the reality of organic, biological life, with all that it contained, stronger and deeper – sometimes even more beautiful – than the subtleties of concealment and subterfuge, and pretensions to delicacy and so-called eminence?

More sincere and reliable, at any rate?

It is simplicity that is demanded now – innocence and openness, with no malicious twisting and turning – in the face of the complexities of half a century of reversals, obscure narrow-mindedness and excuses for the violent repression that attaches itself, with no justification, to religion, law and morality.

So I thought, simple-mindedly.

The earth's horizons extended now over the expanses of the fields, and the gloom of the sunset covered the wide canal, at once vast and constricting. In the all-embracing silence, a breeze stirred, evoking a soft rustling sound from the leaves of the trees, thick and blurry in the twilight of the early evening.

I could hear the voices of the fellahin quite clearly in the distance but I could not distinguish what they were saying.

There was a little wooden boat cutting through the ancient dark waters, without a sound, without a sail, as if it was slipping along on its own with neither boatman nor passengers.

35

On the other bank was a hut made of reeds, dry corn stems and cotton stalks. The doorway looked black to us, in contrast to the pearly light of dusk that was rapidly turning into the dark of evening.

'Have thousands of years really passed?' I asked. 'Are we still in the thickets of Isis?'

Vast expanses of swamp water, a solitary boat guarded by scorpions, is Horus still a lost child promised glory and torment? And you, will you never cease making meaningless comparisons?

The ferry, on its last journey of the day, cuts through the twilight seeking the sun of darkness. Will it ever find it?

Rahma looked at me, a long look it seemed, half a minute perhaps, while Linda chattered incessantly with my uncle Fanus in a low voice, as if she, unusually for her, was afraid of something.

Oh how often I called out in my sorrow, in my loneliness, my beloved! No answer came but my echo, but still I cry, in every valley, and my cry is long! The old man's plaint, the calls of ancient yearnings, the unseen singer's shadow, the playing of the lyre under the protection of snakes, falcons, crows and herds of cattle, awake and asleep alike, forests of laurel and clumps of wild alfalfa sprouting from the salty manure, the fresh, pungent smell of the dandelions between the stems of the wild molukhiya in flower, flocks of white geese winging their way over the canal behind Grandmother Amalia's goose – like a black swan – a goose that we prized dearly and called 'Na'ima', to which she would respond with a cry of acknowledgement. The nymph, the houri, Daphne, my siren, Bride of the Nile, would come to me after leading the flock from the canal to the lanes and alleys of the village, then return home, alone, at each sunset, to eat from my hand the grains of corn, beans, or whatever sustenance God had provided us with.

For a second time, for half a minute.

How much happens – or can happen – in half a minute.

And afterwards, is it not enough?

And then, deep valley where the cave of darkness squats and the temple of dreams smiles, where light mingles with darkness and the small waves clash in the depths of the murky chasm, where the hiss of water rises as if it were boiling, where the gentle rose sings on its quivering branch, kissed with longing by the breeze, showered by the light with love and desire, embraced by the fragrant perfume that rises up from its own depths, then, Oh valley!, what shall be the outcome, where will it all end? A look long as eternity, half a minute, perhaps, a flash of light that appears then disappears in an endless gloom.

On 23 September 1940 *al-Balagh* reported that the body of a woman had been found in the main canal near Kom Bobello. The body had been identified as that of Khadra Mahmud, an inhabitant of Tarrana, in the district of Kafr Dawood. Her corpse was naked, the hair had been shaved and the skull fractured by a blow from an axe. Her family had identified her. They said that she was a bit flirtatious but had never behaved in an immoral way, that she had left five small children and that suspicions centred on her husband, Hegazi 'Awadin who had fled. Enquiries were continuing with a view to arresting him and the public prosecutor's office was in charge of the investigation.

On that day we were about to travel back to Alexandria – we being myself, my sister Aida who died of typhoid a year afterwards, and my sister Hana who ran away some years later, married a Muslim we didn't know and lost touch with me completely. The wind was dry and biting cold as it swept through the dirty, winding lanes, whistling over the threshing floor from which the water had now receded, even though it was still covered in thick mud. In the sky were slow, grey clouds, and there was cold in the bones, a dry, unsatisfied cold.

We didn't go to Tarrana after that, my sisters and I, because after the heavy torpedo attack on the *Piazza* in Bab Sidra and the destruction of Wardiyan and the square between Kom El-Nadura and Sab' Banat Street, we moved to Akhmim in the summer of 1941, and then to Damanhur for the whole of 1942.

To drown is to become a martyr, I said.

So what has become of Linda and Rahma?

Are they still alive, in a country village that has now become crowded and full of the noise of televisions and videos? I know that they left Tarrana some time ago. Could they now be dry, crabby spinsters, reliving the spectacle of Aunt Rosa and Aunt Salome? Or could they be crippled old ladies with children and grandchildren, with cracked, penetrating voices, one of them disabled by illness – or still sprightly, perhaps, constantly on the move like those old ladies who never give up or lose their energy? And how would they look now? Stout, full of folds of flabby, crumpled flesh? Or thin and emaciated, leaning on sticks? Or are they under the ground? That's the fate of us all eventually, isn't it? – a fate that we all know and understand, even though we may choose to forget it, an agony passed from generation to generation.

Disasters striking the heart.

Aside from any possible or probable romanticism, any acceptable or unacceptable nostalgia, Rahma will remain pretty and slim for ever, and Linda will remain tender and physically rebellious.

As for the martyr Khadra, I had hidden her body in my heart, to light for me the path of passion for ever, with a constantly rekindled fire that will never be extinguished, even as the soul is split through fruitless yearning.

What happened to half a minute? What happened to half a century of time?

Will the traces of passion be wiped away?

Will the traces of love be wiped away?

3
Hamida the Leper

Noon in Tarrana is the hour of desolation.

They say that sprites appear in the heat of noon.

The children of Tarrana, though, were not afraid of the sprites appearing. Girls and boys alike, we would sometimes even urge them on, hoping to provoke them and even force them to appear, with a mischievousness that one could understand, perhaps even expect. 'Come on, come out for us then,' we would taunt them as children do, 'won't you come out? The game's up ... !'

Were we really that daring, that naughty, in the black night of Tarrana?

Noon was the hour when al-Khalil, Abraham, met the two angels, and the Lord promised him that a boy-child, her first-born, would be born to Sarah in her old age.

Noon was the hour when Jesus Christ met Saul of Tarsus in a flash of lightning, and Saul became the apostle of Christianity to Rome the glorious, the head of the church and its lawgiver.

At noon also Jesus met the Samaritan woman at the well. He who drinks of this water shall never thirst. When will my thirst be quenched?

At noon He was raised upon the cross and the nails knocked into the wood through the bones of his hands, to save mankind. When will salvation be?

At noon Mu'allim Shenuda the grocer was going back home to his house that overlooked the wide threshing floor in the centre of the village, shaded by an ancient, broad-trunked sycamore tree. He said he had seen something, a woman perhaps, floating in the middle of the Nile. She had a bloated stomach and was lying face down, and her veil, which had turned a dark colour, was spread out on the water, bobbing up and down, half submerged beneath

39

the surface of the waves. He said that he had seen something like a gold star glinting in the sun, with a bright and piercing light. Then the fierce, swirling current had carried her off in the direction of Kafr Dawood, he said. The gold star went with whatever it was that was floating on the current towards the north. 'I swear by God, may He be praised, that it was Hamida the leper,' he said. 'God shame the devil.' Then he crossed himself and praised Christ. The gold star glistened, shining even more brightly at full noon in the heart of the sky. He said he hadn't wanted even to say. A whiff of the decomposing corpse had wafted over him, a strong, greasy smell like no other. 'I could not move until she had disappeared,' he said.

Here I am in the middle. On one side of me there is the cold, dark, cruel, stony half, and on the other side, there is the blazing, molten, shining half. God make me fuel for the burning half, God make me straw for the blazing half! The fire, the fire, I want to stay blazing in the fire!

No.

On the contrary, I want darkness. It fascinates me. I crave its ecstasies and its concealment. I love its deceptions and hypocrisy. I almost yearn for its terrors, for its fears and apprehensions, its dreams and hovering phantoms.

The blind alley connects Aunt Rosa's and Aunt Salome's house to Uncle Arsanius's house, next to ours, under the huge, ancient Christ's thorn tree.

The heat of August fills it with tranquillity and heaviness.

The only sound in this stifling noon is the buzzing of a big blue fly, stubborn, stubbornly defying death, and the crackling of dry, yellowed tree leaves under my feet.

How is it that I find myself in this closed passage that leads to nothing and ends up nowhere? In this baking hour that never finishes, halfway through the day, and the dust.

This funeral pyre, this molten heat, at the false gate of a hell drawn on a blank wall that does not even open onto the bottomless pit but simply blazes with its fire, with no way to penetrate it or fall into it.

The surrounding silence is suddenly broken by the barking of an unseen dog, a long, hopeless sound.

As if he were afraid.

40

As if he were tormented by heat and loneliness.

How can loneliness be submerged in the body's passion?

Can passion banish it, drown it, wipe it out?

Ever?

What is the blazing heat of noon beside the green light of your eyes that flows endlessly into the soul?

My beloved, did you ever exist? Where are you now? Or where am I? Have the hands of time really thrown us apart? Or is our love – my love – too strong for the waves of the night?

Ah, the beat of that naive romanticism that I cannot escape from in the marrow of my bones!

I suddenly saw Hamida the leper at the end of the lane, coming towards me with that slow walk of hers, limping a little.

Where had she come from? The lane had no outlet. Where had she emerged from then?

I sometimes used to see her at Uncle Arsanius's house. Khadra would have summoned her and put her at her ease, patting her shoulder gently, without going very near her. She would have given her some food, leftovers from lunch, molukhiya, okra or purslane, and a tough piece of meat full of bones and gristle in a deep tin bowl – a special one that the rest of us didn't eat from – with a loaf or two of dry pitta bread.

I heard Khadra gently urging her to eat: 'Come on, take it, sister, take it and enjoy it! Easy does it! When did you last eat, poor thing?'

I heard a reply in which the sounds ran into one another, a strange sound, as if receiving compassion like a blow, as if she had lost the power to speak a long time ago. It was a very human sound, however, not an animal sound.

My body shuddered, and I forgot it instantly.

Hamida the leper retreated inside the door, away from the alley dogs and the hungry village cats. With her stumpy fingers she dipped the pitta bread into the sauce and pushed it quickly and eagerly into her cracked mouth. Her swollen, ulcerous lips could hardly close around the piece of food that I could see her swallowing, almost without chewing, as her prominent Adam's apple rose in her throat. Her black veil hung loosely around her, and I could see her eyes rolling with the crazed passion of hunger, and with the enjoyment of satisfying it, but also with the fear of being surprised.

When had she last eaten? And what had she eaten?

I pretend she does not exist, and reject her. Just as everyone in Tarrana denied her existence, refusing to see her, as if she was not there.

The pale blotches on the skin of her face and hands, her thick stumps of half-fingers, the pale, swollen growths on her cheeks and lips, it was these that denied me, curtailed my childhood, and silently said to me: 'No.'

Who knew where she spent the night? Where did she go to sleep? In whose cattle-pen? Under the legs of whose buffalo?

In the early evening she would creep stealthily along, clinging to the walls made of unburned brick, straw and dry durra stalks, hiding her face with the black veil whose grey edges appeared covered with dust and mud.

Khadra said that Hamida the leper, poor thing, never washed her veil or dress until after sundown. She would choose a rough place sloping down to the canal, away from the irrigation channels with their fast-running water from which the earthenware jars were filled, where the birds landed and the cattle and buffaloes bathed, away from the places for washing clothes and washing-up, those places that were chosen and hallowed by the girls and women of Tarrana, who laughed and chattered, flirting with the passers-by as they worked, their bare, brown thighs gleaming with splashes of water, naked, without guilt.

After our return from Wadi al-Natrun, after finishing the supervision of the repaving of part of the desert road (Uncle Nathan had secured the contract from a large contractor whose name I never knew), we were outside Mu'allim Shenuda the grocer's shop in the early evening. Uncle Nathan was there and As'ad Effendi, the son of Uncle Selwanes, the tax-collector's sister, and myself. Shenuda brought out for us two wooden stools with no backs, which Uncle Suryal had made at the beginning of summer. He himself sat on a large white stone, having insisted that Uncle Nathan take the cane chair.

We were facing the shop in the narrow alley, behind us a long, blank, twisting wall with no opening, the wall of Sheikh Alwan's house, the village schoolmaster, imam and reciter at the mosque. Sheikh Alwan used to shield his family from the eyes of the village and he prevented them from visiting anyone, Muslim or Christian,

42

as if erecting a wall around a treasure that was as dry as tinder and as combustible.

His house was on the north side of Tarrana where nearly all the Copts of the village lived, except for two or three families.

The church, however, was on the south side, in the middle of the Muslim houses, in front of the village mansion.

The wide, round threshing floor linked the two halves of the village.

The village mosque was also at the southern end of the village, looking out over the fields on one side and the Nile on the other. The only pump in the village was in the mosque courtyard, supplying the ablutions fountain with clear water in which it was difficult to get soap to lather.

You would come to the mosque after leaving Sheikh 'Isa's farm and the wooden trellis to which clung a wilted, spindly vine over the wide mastaba. You had first to circle the wall of the big mansion, studded with broken glass, potsherds and bits of old jars, and which on its other side rose up directly from the waters of the Nile. No one lived in the large house except for Khawaga Abu Anis, the sole survivor of Dawood's family, and his old servant Hamdan. He also never visited, and no one ever called on him. In fact, he had not opened the wide, wooden door to anyone since his son, a student at the Qasr el-Eini medical school, had come back during his last summer vacation with a dancer from Cairo who he said was a fellow student of his. When Abu Anis came back from Damanhur, he threw his son out of the house but kept the girl. Anis shot himself, and the house had remained completely shut up. From his isolated location, the old man heard only the sound of a single gunshot.

After the big house, you would come to the mausoleum of Sheikh Abu Taqiyya, a green, squat building standing on its own beside the Nile embankment, with an iron window through which we could see the bier, covered in faded green silk. During Friday prayers Shaykh Alwan would light the censer, and people would seek a blessing from the saint.

The last house at the northern end of the village, looking out over the fields beside the old, deserted waterwheel, was Sitt Heneina's house. She had lived there alone since the death of her husband, my uncle Misak el-Banhawi. No one knew the first thing about her, but everyone enjoyed talking about her, especially if they could get their claws into her!

Mu'allim Shenuda invited me to take a glass of arak, which he diluted with water that turned it white, with an oily consistency rather like milk. It had the pungent smell of aniseed. My uncle Nathan urged me to take it and not be embarrassed. 'Take it, son, enjoy yourself! How many times has Uncle Shenuda scrounged a measure of vintage Otard brandy from your grandfather! How many times has he eaten fowl fattened at the hand of your grandmother! Come on, sir, never mind what it costs, you can't take it with you when you die!' As'ad Effendi smiled happily, and the arak went to my head a little, as usual, sharpening my vision, heightening my senses and making my body tense.

When he came back to us from the back of the shop with a quarter of arak in his hand, his heavy steps echoed in the empty space in the middle of the shop.

On the shelves around him, in the semi-darkness, were boxes of tobacco, Coutarelli cigarettes sold by the carton, packet, or singly, rations of tea in small, red, flat, shrivelled paper packets, and other rectangular, square or flexible containers. On the top shelf were whole sugar loaves in their blue paper wrappings; while the broken ones were beside the shop counter, where Mu'allim Shenuda would beat them with a corrugated pound weight, making red sparks fly from the force of the iron striking the lump of pure white sugar. Underneath were packets of salt in grey cardboard boxes with a picture of the Sphinx on them. Beside them were bottles of French oil, with dirt accumulated on the greasy glass, and circles of rough, rolled up loofas. On the other side were cubes of dry yellow Nabulsi Faruq soap that had begun to turn black on the outside. The paraffin containers were beside the door, out of the way, to keep their smell from the other goods. The raw wood shelves were not full. A 'number 5' paraffin lamp gave a feeble glow to the empty space in the middle of the shop. On the dirty floor there were great heaps of corn cobs, sacks of wheat, barley and fenugreek, and dry bettour bread in a big basket. Rows of fresh eggs were arranged in a square basket made of palm leaves. This was the currency of the local people, the village bank. How often did I exchange a corn cob for a kerosene container coupon for my grandmother Amalia, or three eggs for a box of Abu Ghazala tobacco for my grandfather

Sawiris! When Mu'allim Shenuda wanted to go out of the shop he would raise the wooden counter and let it fall back on its two supports with a great crash.

You ordained for me a path on earth, would that I could glitter amidst your essence! Mother of God, possessor of names that cannot be numbered, O my refuge! I do not know you, stranger, I deny you. You are in me at every moment. My troubles are infinite, O mother of villages, you who were born complete and perfect in the shell, O nymph of the mighty ocean, Isis, Astarte, Mary, Rama, pray for me, in the name of lamentations that cannot be spoken. I have buried my face in your darkness that shines with a light that gleams brighter than all the lights of earth and heaven!

The light of my second baptism, the music of the waves, comes from the walls of the tomb under the doum tree. I do not see the sacred monkey but I know that he is crouching motionless between its round, plaited leaves, a prayer of atonement for weighty sins past and future, the dawn of a new moon.

With the mild intoxication of the arak, Hamida's presence passing in front of us under Shaykh Alwan's dark grey wall was powerful, like a threat, in the gentle darkness of the early night. She stooped as she slipped away barefoot, half the toes of her grimy feet fallen off, the remaining stumps thick and swollen. Only her eyes were clear, burning with an inner fire in which there was neither anger nor bitterness. The waves of her soft, flowing hair were carefully combed and brushed under the dirty, faded black veil which spread over her back.

Soft and warm, despite being buried in sand for more than a thousand years. 'May Your name be praised, Jesus!' said Mu'allim Shenuda. 'I was there when I was small, with my father, may God have mercy on him and bless his soul! When they lifted him up,' he said, 'the corpse suddenly oozed blood, and the blood ran over the winding sheets wrapped around him, sheets of yellow linen, like silk they were, as if the wounds of martyrdom were still open and bleeding. The zinc bands around the coffin had disintegrated and the wood of the coffin crumbled as soon as it was lifted into the air. The wood turned into a pale powder like ash, but the signs of the cross drawn on the linen wraps remained, untouched by decay, the patterns of their weave completely undamaged. All those buried around him,' he continued, 'had turned into loose, scattered bones, but the corpse of the martyr had remained whole, his exposed face shining with a light that was not of this earth, as if the spirit had not left him yet. I saw him,' he went on, 'when they exhumed him, before they put him into the new coffin made of expensive walnut wood, secretly, without the government knowing. They said the martyrs' prayer for him one evening by the light of the great candles. The church was packed with people, but not the slightest sound could be heard outside. As the secret Mass reached its climax with the transubstantiation,' he continued, 'I saw him, still physically strong, awesome and full of grace, with traces of indescribable pain etched on his face – pain that he had overcome as he crossed over to Christ, his features soft and clear as he gained the crown of martyrdom.'

'Under Bobello they found the corpse of the priest Basada, which had also preserved its form,' he said.

I said to you, 'I need trees, and people, and heaven with its tranquil waves, and the gulls that soar and screech over the all-engulfing sea, that I may know freedom, that I may free myself from the burden of time with all its glory and its crowns.'

My freedom is not a prisoner within, cut off from the body of the world, from the revelations of the body of God. I take my sacrifice in the broad light of the sun, in the brightness of night with infinite horizons.

No. I did not say that to you.

I did not say it.

I do not say it.

Will this gossip never end? I have counted the cock crow but twice, I still await the third.

Shall I seek the body of the universe, the revelations of the body of God, in your body and its dough?

Or shall I seek your body under the soft skin of the sky, in the muscles of the trees with their yellow flowers that fall on the dust of the road?

'His body was a white colour, quite fresh,' he said. 'Father Andrawus poured over it an expensive new flask of perfume. The entire body immediately turned black, but the limbs stayed supple and fresh. On the shining black face could still be seen dark bruise marks. They had dragged him along the ground as they tortured him, they had flogged him, they had pulled him on his face from the staircase of the governor's palace, they had made him sit backwards on a buffalo, bloody and bruised, and had marched him around the streets of the town.

They had kept him blindfolded the whole time in prison in Tura and Abu Za'bal, put electric wires on his penis, around his testicles and on his nipples, broken his teeth with powerful punches, made him stand naked in cold water, suspended him from his feet until he lost consciousness, as they said: 'Confess ... confess.'

In Peking and Berlin, in Rome and Carthage, in Lourenço Marques and Buenos Aires, in Damascus and Baghdad, in Seoul and Hanoi, they are all the same.

The bruises and disfigurations had become softer through martyrdom, as if they were an added beauty. The arms had been ripped from the shoulder bones, and traces of the boiling pitch poured over his head formed a crown of thorns. The burn marks on his body were untidy belts. Iron pincers had been sunk into his flesh and bones, leaving open hollows in the chest, like perforations from a ship's sharp-pointed anchor, a trinity of torment and martyrdom. Martyrs without name or number, without glory, without monument.

Their lines go on, they fall and are raised again constantly, without ceasing.

In my loneliness – when I face myself – I find my soul always filled with yearning and affection for you, from afar, timelessly. I know that this affection will never reach you. I know that it will tumble uselessly into a void, in the loneliness of the estrangement that has befallen us. Is love, is longing, always lost in vain? And suffering? I do not know. Do you, you, send me love like this, longing like this, compassion like this? Only silence reaches me from you, from them, from anyone.

Old apprehensions of indifference, of a desire to be cut off and to escape.

To escape from confusion, and from doubts and dis-integration.

And a desire – are you entitled to it? – to purify oneself of the bitterness that accumulates from my silence and aloofness that is always our relationship, when we are not together. And sometimes when we are together, also.

Can we rid ourselves of bitterness with pills sold by the chemist like aspirin?

With his harsh, hoarse voice emerging through phlegm from the honeyed tobacco, and small, soggy pellets of opium hidden under his tongue, as he stared with his slightly protruding eyes, obviously short-sighted, through the gloom of the early night, Mu'allim Shenuda's round, fleshy face, pockmarked by fine holes like needle pricks as a result of smallpox a long time ago, would extend itself on his short, solid neck as he strained his eyes forward, and he would tell the story, without the least embarrassment, of Karima, the daughter of Sheikh 'Alwan, his neighbour who never opened his door to anyone.

'Karima would collect old pages from the out-of-date copies of al-Ahram that her father read. When our *'umda* 'Abbas Isawi had finished with them, and after his family had taken them, to help light their stoves and oven, they would then throw them on one side for Hamida the leper to take to Karima. Hamida the leper was the only one who could enter people's houses without permission, for no one could question or approach her. Her leprosy was an impenetrable fortress, a wall around her affording her a unique protection. Karima would cut out with scissors the name 'Muhammad', in small or large point sizes equally, and choose clippings from an illustrated book called New Love Letters by Salim 'Abd al-Ahad, which she would smooth and stick with glue that she made from the bark of the old acacia tree in the courtyard of their house. She did this on Ministry of Education-style exercise book paper, then send them, with Hamida the leper, as love letters to Muhammad, the son of the Sheikh al-balad. She would slip them into old, coverless copies of pocket stories or stories from Ilyas Antun Ilyas's Modern Library, translated by the late Tanyus 'Abduh, with yellowed paper and scuffed corners. She learned to read and write,' he said, 'in primary school in Kafr Dawood when she was living with her mother, who was divorced by Sheikh 'Alwan after various stories had begun circulating about her, unconfirmed though they were, about her having gone behind the mill at sunset (ages ago, of course), and the things that happened there under cover of the alfalfa and scrub, between the women and the village dandies, the ones with no morals.'

The muddy earth sank beneath his feet, his legs slipped in

fresh, welcoming mud, soft to the touch, that drew him to it with an irresistible craving. Were the waters waves of anger or the glistening of a throttled dream, with the taste of salt in his open eyes, her blows gentle but cruel? His breast streamed with painful tenderness as, with her between his arms, he thrust her head in the strange, unresisting element and she yielded to him. The waters rose throwing up no spray until they reached his knees as he pressed on the thin, round, ribbed bone, her mutilated face a copper mask, its surface warm in the dampness, all his defects suddenly atoned for in this gentle swaying; the silky black feathers covered his hands and excited him so that he was suddenly erect without ejaculating. Her black veil spread in the water floating just beneath the ceiling of the waves, neither rising to the surface nor sinking, tossing about with a life of its own; she nestled between his arms as she continued to struggle free, mewing like a grateful plaintive lover. Should he put her under the water with his bare hands? His heart gave a single shout in the face of the floating body and slipped into a still, dark depth at the moment of intimate union with this gentle, nameless being.

Mistress of the khamasin,1 daughter of the dark winter clouds of Tarrana that cast waving shadows, water snakes, my black rose whose thorn's wound on my lips is open and cannot be repaired! I will not bandage it, I said, I will leave the blood to trickle until morning comes unannounced, with the coming of the slave girl of Habi, sacrificed willingly or perforce, a whore untouched by man. Your eunuchs will anoint you with sandalwood and amber and perfumes from behind the stones of Bobello, the pungent smell of frankincense with its enticing stench will encircle your neck, mountains of frankincense and smoke from the sacrifices float up in useless clouds. Stones on stones? I said. For how long will the ruins go on piling up? A soaring dove with clipped wings that does not fall, the butting ram pursues you mercilessly, striking you with horns whose sharp points never break, the buffalo's udders full of doubtful milk, your divine figure is sullied, on the surface of the water float broad melon leaves, dry durra stalks, tossing and turning in the circles of your unseen retinue, times of blessing and of catastrophe, all links broken and all knots undone, the orange blossom holds promise of the game of love on dark benches, the call of wood fires in ovens and stoves.

From afar on the horizon there echoes the whistle of the long express, whose force seems to swallow the fields. 'Eleven thirty, my boys!' says my grandfather Sawiris, accurate as always. 'Another hour and Eryan Effendi the postman will be here, asking for a drink of water from Khadra!'

I saw Hamida the leper coming towards me at the height of noon. Where had she come from? The lane was a dead end, with no way out of it. Where had she emerged from, all of a sudden?

She came straight towards me. Her blazing eyes looked straight into mine. I knew her as a man knows himself.

Alone, no one in the world except her and me, at the silent, lonely hour of noon.

Our bodies met with the force of a collision.

I embraced her with all the yearning and the urge for her salvation that my soul could muster. I did not see her snub, cracked nose, or her pallid, swollen mouth. I folded her in my embrace, as her pungent, penetrating smell submerged me. We were one, a body without divide, in a moment of ultimate abandonment, an unbreakable union.

At first she pulled away from me, like a streak of lightning. Then she came towards me. Only the tremor of the body in a scarcely noticeable gesture of repulsion, and a quivering closeness. I had gone towards her on an irresistible impulse, then composed myself, and she was resigned. I forgot everything.

The closest possible kiss, with nothing between us. Split lips that closed only with difficulty. I could feel their dry skin, sweet in a never-ending process of crucifixion.

She did not shut her eyes, which blazed with a yellow, greenish light. There was no bitterness in them, no anger, no plea for help. There was no victory in them. I saw the depths of my own self in those eyes.

In a sort of daze I saw in her dainty ears a small earring, a golden star that glinted in the sun and then was gone. Her body in my embrace was a surprise, soft and pliant. I could feel that she was not wearing anything under her faded black galabiya, and her flesh was tender, fresh and virginal. I felt them, two strong breasts on my own breast, almost hard. All at once I knew a total detachment from the world, a complete union with this warm body.

Then we parted, without a sound.

50

I said, 'a mask'. What guilt can a man be punished for when the body's mask is imposed on him?

The mask shames, ruined stones.

She said: 'You are taller than any of them.'

She said, no, it was not she who said it: 'Are you so romantic? Much bigger than you.'

As if the disfigured mask had never been.

I said, 'That means nothing, anything. It neither confirms nor disproves anything.'

I said, 'Have you become one of the gods?'

I will not offer my sacrifice, then. My complaint.

Every year, Habi lifts your small, tender breasts before him, two succulent fruit.

The Nile gives you its pure water, now polluted by factory refuse, chemical waste and animal excrement.

As for the pure narcissus flowers, you have adorned your flowing hair with them, rubbing it with olive oil, bees' honey and buffalo milk, and in summer with the undiluted wine of the grape.

Your hidden femininity and your secret masculinity are two inseparable elements in the essence of your love that blazes in the glass of deep-red cognac which I never cease from drinking with the beloved, never overflowing, never full. The beats of the small drum and the tambourine's whisper in a wedding not yet begun, do you anticipate their taste? Struck by bow and arrows, your shattered head is drowned in a baptismal font that never runs dry, the threshing floor of Tarrana whose Nile waters have dried up now, and whose memory has gone. The cries of love's triumph, the shouts of the lover's orgasm of wasted sperm, the tenderness of the basil and the sandy texture of the wild geranium are all hidden together under ruins and turpitude on the edge of the western desert, under the protection of Bobello, spread out unendingly, your ancient child who never came, your Adonis, your Horus, your Jesus, your Guevara, all, all of them thrown down, none flourished until the ultimate plenitude, nor wilted.

You have become numbered among the gods: therefore I shall not offer my sacrifice or my complaint.

Bride of the sea, buried under a misshapen mask, I have built my inner being for you as a house and a firm refuge that will never collapse or be destroyed. An intrusive mask, what is behind it?

51

A fragile shell. The mask and what is behind it become one. One, they are the single result, with no duplication, are they not?

I feel it as a lofty castle though I know that it is a thing of no value, whether a prayer-niche, a sanctuary, a dwelling-place of sin, or none of these things, but the abode of a vulgar, possibly trivial nightmare in the blazing noon in a cul de sac in a shabby village that has changed, gone and vanished.

This lamentation has the ring of wisdom and depth and poetry, it seems to be filled with the wisdom of years. I say, to myself, of course, 'Hey? Do you think that? Heavens! But at the end of the day it is slightly comic, common, vulgar, and repeated to the point of boredom, isn't it?'

The firewood of poetry is brittle and dry, unfit even for lighting fires.

The net of words is broken, it will hold nothing. The fish fall through, returning dead to the sea. I have no net. The net and the fish are the same.

A shell with a narrow opening, hollow, round and soft-bellied, ringing with an unreadable, inexplicable hum.

4

An Upper Window with Blue Glass

When a man wakes from a noon siesta to find the afternoon sky broad and firm in its soft blueness, with the wind wafting from the heaven to the soul – in such a moment of gentleness, this life seems beautiful and calm. The sun is warm but not hot, not oppressive, and children are playing and shouting in the busy street.

When a man finds this gentle sky, with the swift birds soaring in it, soaring, circling, then swooping down over the sunlit houses, and finds that all this world equals nothing but the beauty of a moment, the twisting of the gentle breeze, the fluttering of birds' wings, the bustle of the city swimming in the afternoon sun, then a man can for a moment feel peace passing through his heart, inspiring him with a gentle humility, a resignation and acceptance of tragedy (without being resigned to it), a sorrow in which there is now no revolt, no tears, no irony and no rage, but rather silence like that which comes with beautiful music.

How I would like to find, on my path, a few more of these moments, the peace that meets beauty in the sky, which meets the silence of loneliness in which there is no anger, untroubled by the meaning of tragedy or the weariness that afflicts the lives of thousands and millions who live in the grinding dust of life, uncorrupted by pernicious, parasitic extensions of apprehensions and forebodings.

But they are rare, these moments.

Five or six years ago I used to go every afternoon to a forgotten sandy island in the Nile, an island which surfaced every year and was then submerged by the flood, before being uncovered again. I would sleep on the sand after sunset, my eyes fixed on this same blue sky, deep blue in the twilight. I dreamed of a great love, a 'noble' love, I called it, of deep-rooted friendships to challenge the misfortunes of time, of lofty deeds, of castles in the air. At that time I did not know peace, or so I thought. I did not know the meaning of a man's acceptance of tragedy. Do I know it now? As I recall, I used to slope off into a dark corner, in the locked room in my grandfather Sawirus's house, or into a dark corner of the soul, one or the other, and I would cry like a child whose heart has been rent by stormy, ungovernable blows. Wasn't I – aren't I still – that child? I would cry because Rahma or Linda (did I know which? Did I? I believed I was in love with her, do I not still believe that I love one of them, both of them?) had not been gentle with me, and did not know me. (My demand for affection and knowledge is never-ending, unfortunately.) And because no one in the whole universe knew the secrets of my dreams, because no one could love moonlight as I loved it, or listen with me to the roar of the waves on the Nile, or to the clamour raging within me.

Or so I thought.

But the crying was genuine, and very painful.

In the darkness of my tears I knew inside myself that loneliness was unbearable, and that silence was devastating, and never ending.

In the afternoon, then, I would leave small, dusty Tarrana for this sandy island of mine, which seemed to have been invented for me. I would rush off in the heat of the afternoon sun, unable to bear the stagnation of the hot village and the insistent, monotonous whistling of the mill, which shrieked, then grew silent in the emptiness, silent then shrieking, silent then shrieking, continuous and stubborn as if it had been seized by madness. What did I care that people were milling their wheat and barley and fenugreek, and that life was anyhow hard?

I would escape, almost running, to the ancient bosom of the Nile, crossing the shallow ford, lifting the hem of my galabiya with my sandals in my hand, careful not to trip in a deep hole and wet my clothes, feeling for a place for my feet across the clear, sparkling water.

I would wander on the sandy island, no one there but myself, nothing but the summer plantings of watermelons ripening slowly on their own. I would stare, fascinated, at the great, green fruits, almost sunk into the sand, hidden under the broad, creeping foliage. I chose a (small) one once and crushed it in my hands. It disintegrated easily. I dug my teeth into it, it was half sweet but not completely ripe. I threw the peel away with all the strength I had, into the deepest part of the Nile I could reach.

I would pace around my island, my bare feet sinking in the soft, white sand, then run after the blue birds that flew low, chasing them. They seemed to be within reach, that I had only to stretch out my hand to catch them, but they got away from me (don't they always get away?) – an image flying in a dream, racing, fleeting impressions, blue and beautiful, flying low as if to deliberately entice me. I would run after them, knowing now that I would never catch any of them. I simply liked to run after them, filling my eyes and my soul with them, and with the heaven to which they suddenly soared, descending from it swiftly and silently – blue, living songs thrown down from the sky.

When I had exhausted myself and was completely out of breath, I would throw myself down on the white sand and begin to dig with my hand in the sands until water appeared, little lakes of clear water in the holes in the sand. I would build my childish dams and bridges around them, I would fill up the lakes, then make others, dreaming, now that sunset was about to overtake me, that there were small red lights appearing from Tarrana, across the Nile embankment.

In those days I did not know the meaning of peace.

Do I know it now? Did I ever know it?

My heart was full of dreams, some childlike in their nobility and innocence, others harsh, ugly dreams that sprang from the soul's passion and the fervour of a body that was striking against the cocoon of youth and plunging into the first waves of masculinity.

Now, as the Alexandrian breeze in Raghib Pasha becomes a little stronger, as the sky turns a deeper, matchless blue, and the day declines towards sunset, I no longer feel this peace except in passing – a guest who gives a greeting from the street, then goes off, like the three angels who visited the patriarch Abraham, ate under his tent, gave him good tidings, then went on their way. The Lord was among them.

At midday I would return with Shafiq Busturus, Ahmad Sabri and Wadi' Butrus. I would feel the old, stubborn heaviness weigh down my soul, a heaviness in everything, leaving only a stagnation that weighed on my heart. They would laugh those perverse laughs of theirs, sighs of a misery that wants to escape from itself, groans of self-assertion of a soul absorbing its life's breath from the heart of life's crush, sighing and laughing because it finds around it such perverse relationships between people and things – all those ridiculous beings (some large, some small) sticking out their tongues in a man's face and rolling their eyeballs in front of him.

In this we were following the same old path that we had marked out for ourselves amid the rubble and remains of immature thoughts, perverted relationships, and sterile images. No one cares, no one will ever care, what happens or will happen, what happened or did not happen. Each one of us – whatever he may tell himself – treads an improvised path, each one of us is alone in himself with his own dreams and laughter and sighs, alone forever, alone like a condemned man. Alone, in the end concerned with no one, interested in no one. Right?

Wasn't friendship and companionship (and love?) supposed to put an end to this loneliness? Why then do these ties make loneliness harder to bear?

In my loneliness, and in rare moments of peace, I would always feel that he was with me. But he bore the weight of his (*his*) loneliness to the end, with his own hand banished his burden, and disappeared.

A bullet from a small revolver like a toy: I am fleeing from misery. '*I saw her this morning, ran my hand through her hair and touched her brow with my lips. She felt what was in my soul, her eyes flickered, I was afraid I would cry. Never leave her, Badawi, keep her for my sake, for she is unhappy and I adore her. Munir. Friday 20 May 1945. I am fleeing from misery.*'

As for me, I do not have this option.

I can only look at the moment of escape from misery as a man looking at one of his old dreams. It will not be fulfilled through his will. This last moment is not in my hands. I must wait in silence, working, and sobbing with laughter. I would chase blue birds that I would never catch, then throw myself down in the sunset twilight, exhausted but still dreaming. And at night, wretched and lonely, I would cry in the darkness.

As the policeman said to the criminal when he finally caught him, and he complained and burst into tears:

'Poor fellow ... you have broken my heart ...'

I would press her smooth, small neck with all my power,

clinging to every curve in it with all my resolve, happy somehow or other in her damp embrace. We would float together, interlocked, in a single wave motion, her flesh firm beneath my hands, a new fresh tenderness in it. In the darkness of the water a single gold star gleamed, tossing with the waves' slow trembling. The water was shallow and constricting. We thrashed about with our arms without splashes. I did not believe my eyes, even though I knew at the bottom of my heart that it was inevitable. 'To drown is martyrdom, to burn is martyrdom,' I said. A bead sparkled in the little ear, still clean, somehow retaining its unsullied appearance in the pondweed. The water rises over my head, rises until it reaches the clouds in the sky, my arms encircle her body. I carry her down clutching her to my breast. There is no escape from the kiss now, I taste its earthy flavour, it has a silent, gentle sweetness. I love this immersion, I do not flee from it, it has taught me, through my loss of you, that we love alone as we shall die alone. My feet sank in the soft mud with a silence from which I did not emerge.

No, I would go out at noon, plodding along narrow, earthen tracks between fields of durra, cotton and clover. The smell of warm greenery would fill me, as I walked without end or purpose, turning and twisting with the lanes, the fields of wheat tall and full of stalks heavy with leaves and slowly ripening ears, in the earth, so tall and close that I almost sank in the wilderness of the fields through which I could scarcely cut a path. I would pass waterwheels beside the small canals, and others on the bank of the main canal, whose water was low, slow-moving and a little greenish, seeping away under the embankment into the parched earth of the unirrigated land in the blazing noon. Until I reached the Nile.

I would race down a slope from the river embankment, so fast that I almost fell. I knew this spot in which the shallow waters glistened, clear and blue in their transparency. I would take off my slippers and hold them in my hand with the edge of the galabiya that I lifted well above my knees, plunging into the water without disturbing the sand on the soft, firm riverbed. I saw my feet broken from the play of the light at the almost glass-like water's edge, I would go up with the river bed little by little until I reached the shore of the island that I suddenly believed was mine, where I walked, completely alone and in silence, a silence embellished only by the rippling of the water that was soaking into the sand by the deep, nearer bank, turning it dark. On the other side of the shallow ford by which I had crossed, the breezes blew in the middle of the Nile, damp, warm and sweet, with an almost sugary taste that was in some way intoxicating.

Suddenly I would stop, and with furtive footsteps steal up on a blue bird with long wings whose name I did not know. I would walk towards it nimbly and silently, trying to catch it. Suddenly it would fly up in front of me, with steady, blue wings and feathers that scarcely moved, almost transparent. Then suddenly a whole flock of blue birds was soaring with it, heading for the other shore, rising aloft to the heavens, their emerald feathers waving as they flew together, flapping noiselessly, an explosion of dreams and desires and loves as yet unknown, that I had never yet grasped.

Phantoms knocked on my door, I did not open for them, but desire made me excited and disturbed.

I knew that I would be worn out and exhausted by your shadow that came to me night and day, bringing me grief and sadness, but what was I to do? Should I bear it, exhausted as I was? Or summon it? No, I do not like suffering, I cannot bear pain coming near me. How much worse, then, if it surrounded me and would not go away?

'I was long detained', the victim of beauties or the victim of hovering desires.

What could I give you? How could I stretch out to you the hand of love, in your loneliness, perhaps in your astonishment?

Uncle Mikha'il would say to me: 'I came to her and she came to me when the day was nearly over. After I had spent my lifetime on land that was not hers, nor mine either, for I have no land and no refuge. After my hands were about to become empty of everything, with no sorrow and no pain.'

He will say to me, 'There is only this strange love that fills the furthest, locked room of the house, the fortieth room.'

What use is it to you? What support could you find in it? I want to give you security, help and succour. But I do not know whether you are really in need of it. Unwanted, perhaps unnecessary help.

Etc, etc.

I will say, 'The first kiss is also the last kiss, perhaps?'

The healing kiss is also the kiss of final destruction, perhaps?

Perhaps I shall say, or not say, 'The man who said this is a man who loves you, you, when you were an expected or anticipated existence, before and afterwards. In his eyes you are a tangible, overwhelming presence. You, when you are a consummation, an impossibility, a pining in my bosom, a dream, a memory and a delusion, and a daily vulgarity, all at the same time.'

Your presence that is yours alone.

Like the shadow of a black cat under my window.

I said, 'Where does she sleep?'

By the doors? In the earthen courtyard? In the open air? Or in a soft, warm bed, especially made?

During the last days of the drought, when the Nile waters rose up at that point of the river, if I lifted my galabiya as far as my waist and waded into the water so that it wet my underwear, I could cross to the other bank. I would pant from the adventure in a darkness that was now imminent, careful to tread in exactly the right place lest my legs sink into the hollows of the river bed that I could not now see through the surging water.

I would return from my adventure that no one knew about, exhausted, dirty and wet. I forgot to eat, and I forgot the reception I would receive from Grandmother Amalia. 'Oh dear, oh dear! Why is your face so pale, my child? You're as white as a sheet! Oh my God! What am I going to do with you, Ibn Sausan? What on earth are your mother and father going to say? ... . Come on, child, calm down, be quiet, how long will I have to go on shouting? Change your clothes and get something to eat!'

She would clasp me in her scrawny arms, arms as wide as the affection of the whole world, as she brought me a pitta loaf, fresh and warm, with newly made butter melting on its fragrant, reddish surface.

As I was coming back that night, I took the long way round behind the mill, so as not to have to walk through the fields. Darkness had fallen, there was an eerie barking of dogs, and a sort of howling in the distance that curdled the blood. How could I tell what it was? Was it the howling of hyenas, or the yelping of a wolf?

In the brush and luxuriant alfalfa behind the mill, I sensed a familiar presence.

I heard her lecherous moans and stifled shouts: 'Ah!...oh dear, oh how ominous is the night! Careful, my dearest, gently, don't hurt me, my love, Oh, don't clutch so hard, my lad, may you be

59

grabbed by disaster, Oh, poor me!', and the groans of the man, panting with a hoarse, rough sound. The sounds of the night and of lechery, the moans of snatched pleasure and the raucous harshness of ecstasy seemed to me more frightening than the howling of wild animals whose names I did not know.

She caught up with me from behind the mill and overtook me. I could not see her face in the darkness, but she did not seem embarrassed in the way she walked, or look sheepish – nothing, very natural she seemed to me, physical satisfaction unaware, even, of being satisfaction, or contentment or fulfilment. It was the body itself, taken for granted, unconscious, and no need to give it a second thought. The basket of flour on her head was balanced by the rhythm of her calm, confident steps. Her veil was covered with dust – white flour dust and pale dust from the earth on the ground (I noticed this quickly). Her bearing was upright, and she seemed unconcerned, like someone who has just finished a job or performed a task and is at peace. She had not a care in the world.

I had come back from Tarrana that year, and the poems of Shelley and Keats were keeping me company in the room overlooking Gulnar Alley. I had by this time forgotten its small high windows, directly under the roof, glass skylights with no frames, with white, yellow and turquoise-blue glass. From them a constant sky-blue light filtered through to the room, a soft, special light, diffusing a friendly tranquillity and pleasant atmosphere. This room now seems to me quite poor and threadbare, but not unattractive; indeed, I love it with all my heart.

At night the light from the street lamp softened its harshness, of which I was not even conscious. My poetry softened its edges and made it friendlier.

In this light, by night and by day, I wrote my first poems on my old marble table, its worn wooden legs scarred by old woodworm from long ago with lots of tiny holes. Its grey-white marble, oval shaped, with twisted veins, still exists to this day. The long sofa covered with rough, coloured cushions over a cotton mattress, slightly hard, is exactly as it was forty or fifty years ago. Today it is slept on by Mutawalli Mabruk, the milkman who delivers the milk on the streets of Gheit El-'Enab and Ragheb Pasha – milk in containers large, medium or small, in old-fashioned colours, hung carefully on the bicycle that he props under the stone staircase that

60

has replaced the wooden one under which I often waited in the darkness for Mona – Mona with the thick lips and jutting tooth under her upper lip, how often did I dream of a kiss on her soft, wide, passionate mouth! I never knew it, this kiss, but I knew death and parting and rejection – all natural, ordinary, expected and familiar, with neither hue nor cry.

At the door I would hear the woman shouting at her neighbour in the alley, looking out from her window that faced my old, glass windows, swearing as loud as she could, 'I'll be damned if it was me that threw the melon rind your son (God bless him!) slipped on, my good woman. Melon? It didn't even come into our house this year!' When I ask her whether she remembers the people who lived in this house fifty years ago, Umm Mahmoud and her daughters Gamalat and Mona, she laughs in a quite inappropriately flirtatious way, with her toothless mouth, just the stumps of molars visible, and says: 'Goodness me ... fifty years? Do you think I'm an old woman, or what? It's just worry that's worn me out, my friend. Mona? Gamalat? Umm Mahmoud? Never seen them, never known them. People that know you never forget you!'

From her upper window, the neighbour, her ample bosom spilling out tight against the window frame, shouts sharply to the child, who is running away from her in the alley: 'Hey, you, child, wasn't it you that saw Umm Sayyid throw the melon rind? Answer me, child, may you choke! Wasn't it you that said it?'

He had lifted his galabiya up to reveal a dark-skinned, naked bottom, and run off in the direction of the street where – as we watched, amazed – Nafisa had lain down, mimicking with all the eloquence of her body the story of Mona's lovemaking and the pantomime of the birth of an imaginary child.

As for the high bed with the posts and the curtain worked in lace, it was in its place, and still is. As if my father would be coming in late tonight and staying up with his measure of glowing brandy and a snack of sliced boiled eggs with lemon squeezed over them, with some Turkish cheese, and a little piece of chicken. He would then go up to his half-night, and his loving, on this bed, while I would stay up in the inner room that looked out over the light shaft, studying, reading selections from the *Sihah*[1], translating poetry, seeing lakes of blue, icy water and green meadows stretching to the horizon, with Hamida the leper's kiss still on my lips, making me shiver and burn.

With the power of this moist earth, its fertility deeply ingrained, you subject both men and gods to your authority.

Are there spells and talismans in the amulet that my uncle Shaykh 'Ulwan wrote for you with onion juice, and red and blue ink, with a reed pen, on thick textured paper, folded into triangles one on top of the other? Do you draw them towards yourself, submissive, enchanted, with closed eyes and passions guarded?

In Thomas Lawindi's garden you make the guava fruits fall. Your two prize pomegranates ripen to the point of rottenness before anyone can savour their juice. The red berries hang down from the split mouth.

You who guard Thebes, in fragrance, always fresh and soft and scorching, again, for greedy lips, in the radiant blindness of their lust.

You who read fortunes in the sand, whispering to the sea shells, your nose pierced with rings of jagged copper.

I said, 'I safeguard your pride.'

Daughter of the red Negus of Abyssinia, sprung forth from the silt of the Nile before time.

As she rose from the shell of darkness, raising her arms, her pale, black veil had slipped from her shoulders, and the thin, white collarbone appeared through the gaps in the dress she was wearing over her flesh, as she implored the love of music that she would never hear, even though she had known it deeply from remotest eternity.

I refute you, Begetter of the light, in the darkness of my sky under the palm tree where you were born, under your olive tree, I negate my refuge, I refuse my refuge, your horizons have carried me around, but their barriers are too narrow, the bird of the heart is slaughtered on living water; my blood your blood drips pure and polluted one time then another in a smooth, shining earthenware bowl that has just emerged from the oven.

With my right hand I splash a sprinkling of warm water on the face smitten with an eternal kiss.

My birds have flown away on their blue wings, soaring in the vastness of the heavens that are closed for seven days and seven nights – no nest to shelter in, their exile never ending.

The bleating of the Redemptive Lamb is answered by an echo

that bears the bleating, like two angels, two young doves, to your sun that puts a drop of chrism oil on my right ear, on my right thumb, on my right big toe, pure, pure, pure, what is left of the oil you rub on my head, I have no need of it, I shake it from me, I refuse it, I light a fire of the tatters of my soul, I do not want its smoke to rise up to You, no, it turns to come back inside me.

Will the music of the golden lyre, the music of the reed pipe, or the flute, wash away the filth of union with the Nile's bride in her watery death, her stomach bloated in death?

Despite everything, there is never any purification, for purity has existed from eternity, untouched by the stains of anger or subservience.

What do you suppose has been decreed for the heart?

The thorns of grief, or the fragrance of love?

Was it the Plaza cinema, or the Cosmo cinema? Was this the scene of the long, iron fence whose legs, like spears, followed one another under the light of the projector that moved on a trolley, a round patch of light amidst the darkness, casting a succession of shadows on what seemed to be empty fields or vast, deserted gardens? The tearful voice seared my soul, he being still a child. Oh my love, oh my suffering, oh my grief, hope is lost for my love ... Why was the young boy crying in the darkness of the cinema? I sacrificed my love, for your happiness ... What love, ravished and destroyed in the heedlessness of youth, in the thrill of emerging adolescence, and the breakdown of the soul in maturity, all at once?

What delusions are these that have been with you, and are with you still, since that time long ago?

Are you really a person who has wasted his life in delusion?

Or as he said?

I will not give in ... give in ... to the temptation of despair ...

No ... I will not give in ...

Give in ...

Not give in ...

No ...

5

The Collapsed South Wall

One warm early morning in Misra,1 when the Nile had risen and covered the threshing floor, I saw Mu'allim Gorgi coming towards us, raising his head, as they all did. He was striking the ground rhythmically with his stick, feeling his way with it expertly and confidently, though his appearance as he crossed under the broad Christ's thorn tree in front of grandfather Sawirus's house was ominously agitated. He stood at the door and shouted, 'People of God … Ba Sawirus!'

Before going in, feeling his way over the threshold with his stick carefully and eagerly, he knocked the two sides of the entrance with his stick and passed through the wide wooden door.

With his full, baritone voice he said, as loud as he could: 'The south wall of the church collapsed today, early this morning.'

He said that he had seen the angel of the Lord, yes, he had seen him, he had seen him shining in his glory. He had struck the wall a single blow with his sharp sword. Glory be to God! A single blow had passed through the heart of the great, stone wall. Quickly, and gently.

Fire was blazing on the edges of the broad sword, I felt its flame as I was lying in the outer, southern courtyard: 'Isn't that right, Ba Sawirus?'.

He said that he had felt the heat of the fire before the great sword was raised, then he saw it. He saw the surface of the sword stretched out and gleaming, mellow, with small balls of fire running over its surface, skating over it with a hissing sound. Then he heard the thud of the decisive blow.

'Oh Abu Arsani, the blow was for me, for me, me!'

He said that he had heard the stones of the massive old wall falling, crashing down with a series of thuds like thunder. When

64

I stood up straight and walked south the morning breeze was blowing warm straight onto my face and I learned from the priest that the marble column on which the wall had been built had leaned to one side, taking with it the wooden cupboard with the old Book of Martyrs inside it, bound in its original leather binding, and the blessed pictures and icons, with the Coptic and Arabic gospels, it had disappeared under the stones, under the heap of rubble that had risen all at once higher than my stick would reach. Lord, have mercy. Kyrie eleison.

He said, 'I saw him seize the capital of the massive column, like a mighty millstone, carved and inscribed with ancient script. I saw him', he continued. 'He threw it with a single arm thrust towards the Nile. I heard the noise as it struck the water, and its spray reached me; it fell in the river, and a huge fountain rose up and the chasm that it left as it fell remained open. I saw it, the waters did not return to their origin, and like the reaper with his scythe the angel of the Lord said in a mighty voice: "Thus shall Babylon, the mighty city, be cast down, and shall not exist hereafter. Thus shall I hurl all the sinners into an open chasm."

He said, 'The Gospel alone will heal the broken and restore the ruined.' When he took off his dark glasses for a moment, his eyes were bulging and their whites were pale as they turned without direction, without focus. He put on his glasses again at once.

We only realised it some hours later, when some fellahin stumbled by chance on my uncle Basili stretched out motionless and shattered under the ruins, unconscious and covered by large stones, so that we thought there was no hope for him.

When they carried him to the small mud building in the courtyard of the church, Father Andrawus prayed for him, and he opened his eyes, nothing more. In a vague and uncertain voice he said: 'Gorgi. My brother!' After that he did not speak again. Only his eyes shone, though his right eye had stopped motionless in its socket, its lid heavy. His arms hung lifeless by his side, and his legs were both paralysed. Despite myself, I surprised him in Sitt Hunaina's room, stiff and lifeless, at the end of the summer. The following summer I found out that he could walk, with difficulty, leaning on an improvised crutch, roughly fashioned from a strong sycamore branch.

Mu'allim Gorgi did not know that his brother had got up from his bed in the morning and that the south wall of the church had fallen on him. The angel of the Lord had struck him as though to punish him for a sin that he had not committed; is this the fate of the innocent?

My uncle Basili, that good, vigorous, energetic man, it was he who with his sturdy arms undertook the cultivation of the two qirats left by his father, the old Aba Wingate Darbas, providing a secure income for himself and for Uncle Gorgi. Now, he could no longer stand upright.

Mu'allim Gorgi's face was flushed and red, pinched and bloated with skin that was originally a dark colour, pockmarked from an old smallpox infection. His bulging eyes were split and raw, and his eyeballs revolved without seeing, though despite that you felt that they were following you, and watching every movement, even inside your soul. Only now, they no longer had that sense of defiance, shamelessness and ribaldry that the whole of Tarrana had been aware of and accepted in him (approved of, even) for some time. Rather, a sense of alarm, and foreboding, and recognition of guilt.

None of this had anything to do with the fact that he was the church precentor and senior sacristan, that he had memorised perfectly the liturgy and a thousand Coptic and Arabic chants, and that he was there whenever anything happened, great or small, for childbirth, baptism, engagement celebrations, marriage ceremonies or funeral rites, for the sprinkling of holy water forty days after death to relieve the soul of the burden of separation and set it free in peace, for exorcisms, for celebrating the arrival of a new-born baby, eating the body of Jesus and drinking his blood, at the signing of contracts of sale and rent, after the cotton harvest, at the weighing of the wheat, at the slaughtering of the goose, and the mating of the buffalo, at games of backgammon, dominoes and cards, and when the local physician (or equally, the station officer) came, when things got tough. His presence on every occasion (and on none at all), with his closed eyes and the smack of his greasy lips, his obscene comments and filthy stories, openly expressed in plain Arabic, gave everyone a feeling of peace with him, of pleasure in him, even – a slightly dubious pleasure, perhaps, but allowed and accepted because it was basic, like the pleasure that surprises your hands and body when you grasp the contours of your wife, full and rounded like leavened dough, and plunge into the night.

The whole of Tarrana, without exception, spoke always with pleasure and sometimes with a sense of scandal about the fact that Mu'allim Gorgi could be seen (how could he fail to be seen?) with his frightening frame and tapping stick, going alone and unabashed into Sitt Hunaina's house (she also being alone and unabashed) in the middle of the night, after sunset, that is, and how he was seen by the fellahin heading for their fields in the freshness of the early morning, by children grazing their cattle, and women carrying their clay pots and earthenware jars in a happy procession to the waters of the irrigation canal under the Nile embankment, where the water flows clear and restores the spirit. They can all testify that he emerged from her house before sunrise heading for the church and his mud room that Father Andrawus had built for him. God have mercy on you, 'Amm Misak Banhawi, you die of a terrible disease – may the name of the cross protect us! – and leave this woman to use her body shamelessly, blazing with her passion for life, alone and childless. You could leave her no offspring, but you left for her the six feddans and the two qirats in Uncle Thomas's garden.

My uncle Silwanus the tax-collector always used to say, 'Come on, people, leave her be, those of you that have no sin ...'

And Grandmother Amalia would say, simply and insistently, 'May our Lord forgive me on the Day of Judgment. This woman never stopped acting like a whore. Can adultery be covered up? There are three things that can't be hidden – passion, pregnancy, and riding a camel!'

My grandfather Sawirus would restrain her gently, saying that she should leave judgment to the Lord of Judgment. 'God alone can forgive sins, through the intercession of our Lady Mary and the saints. The Son of Man and his inheritors on earth also have power. Faith redeems, Umm Yunan.'

And Father Arsani would say, with a stern look and unsmiling cheeks, 'Umm Yunan, it was Mary Magdalene who lived in sin that poured the bottle of perfume over the feet of Jesus, and wiped his feet with her hair. Jesus forgave her, and she was the first person to whom he appeared after his bodily resurrection.'

She would answer him without malice, and even without offence, 'Sisters! Oh, you men!'

Did she mean that Jesus was also a man?

We went to church next Sunday morning, to attend Mass and take communion, and to see the collapsed wall with our own eyes.

We walked through the narrow, twisting lanes of Tarrana, under old palm-trees with leaning trunks, ancient sycamores, camphor trees with cracked stems, and houses of ancient mud.

Linda and Rahma, and my aunts Rosa and Salome, were walking a few steps in front of us, though the bends in the lanes and unexpected courtyard walls would hide them from us for a moment, then, as if by some morning magic, suddenly reveal them again directly in front of us.

I was walking behind them, with my aunts Sarah and Wadida, and a solemn grandfather Sawirus, his thick, strong-knotted stick tapping the earth and stirring up a light dust with every blow. Sitt Amalia stayed at home preparing Sunday lunch, special food cooked in fat.

Linda's yellow dress, decorated with patterns of delicate red flowers, flowed down over her. I was surprised and aroused, despite the morning hour, by the way it hung almost tight over her thighs, then spread out into a sort of ledge underneath, with a wide border immediately above her feet. She moved vigorously and alertly, and it was obvious that she was not used to walking in her expensive, brown, men's shoes. She always wore wooden sandals, and sometimes went barefoot, boldly and without shame.

She was a little behind the women's magic procession, when she threw me a quick, conspiratorial glance. Or so I imagined.

The peasant children looked at us with childish curiosity, and an instinct for mischief that was only held in check by the presence of grandfather Sawirus, with his tall, lofty frame, not looking at anyone.

Falling stones had already blocked the back lane behind the church and cut off the road to the big house. Children were climbing on the high, unsettled heap, calling out in happy, excited voices, and going down in the opposite direction under the wall of the church nave, from the outside.

The great gash that had split the south wall in two had been closed up with a large sheet of tent canvas, the sort from which wedding and funeral pavilions are made. Father Andrawus had brought it from Kafr Dawood, decorated with red and blue arabesque designs. In the middle of each pattern of branches the name of God was repeated in slightly grubby white stitching, the threads of which were thick and slightly prominent. The cloth was held up by slightly leaning wooden planks, which hid the heap of stones. From around it daylight filtered through from outside, making a strange, worldly frame around the edges of the cloth in the darkness of the broad church nave. The haloes from the big, solitary candles emphasised the flimsy, otherworldly texture of this darkness. Among them were smaller candles, singly and in groups, crowded together, suspended in ancient, wooden chandeliers that were split with the lines of age.

The few men among us were on the right of the church. The women had covered their heads with headscarves and veils, and despite the heat they all wore long sleeves. Their dresses were long and loose-fitting, and the shadows of their eyelashes in the gentle light of the candles spread over their tender cheeks, softening the dryness of the bones of the old women.

Oh Lord, You know my weakness and my shortcomings and my sins, support me and support all sinners by Your grace, help me and strengthen me and all sinners with Your power; if I fight alone and triumph over Satan alone, I may be prey to the fault of pride and vanity, I may fall into the pit of fire that has no bottom and disappear in the depths of the open sea; clothe me, Lord, in the garb of piety and make me to wear the loincloth of chastity; Lord, of your great mercy, cover me with your blessings that I may know the poverty of my soul and the impurity of my heart and the evil of my nature, for if I fall without help, I may be prey to the ravenous eagles of despair, with no escape, so grant me to fix my eyes on you to eternity; were it not for your mercy I shall not escape from the poverty of my soul; Lord, have mercy, *Kyrie eleison, Kyrie eleison*.

I said, he was praying for himself. No. For her, for me, for Uncle Gorgi, for us, for us all.

I said, they are not my prayers, they are not my supplications. My refuge is the pride of my sins whose worth I know not.

Linda had cheeks flushed with the fire of prayer. I knew that she rubbed her tender face with a red taffeta cloth until her cheeks were red, that she bit her lips and coloured her eyes with kohl with a fine-edged silver stick from a bulbous kohl jar of constantly bright silver, while Khadra, with a woman's connivance, helped her to wrap herself her plait around completely so that her luxuriant black hair looked as though it was suddenly spilling out over the tender skin of her face.

As I stole a glance at her in the church, however, I was convinced that her red colour was divine, that she was red from the fire of the Coptic and Arabic prayers, and from the rhythm of Mu'allim Gorgi's chants, with his deep voice that filled the nave of the church and made the candles' flames flicker, skin and heart both straining towards it together. His rough face, pocked with the marks of an old smallpox attack, seemed serene and full of light.

I saw (or did I imagine it?) her teardrops, shining, perfectly round and crystal clear, as they fell slowly on the soft, blazing cheek.

The church dome was high, way out of reach, wooden, naked and dark, yet despite that perfectly round. It was supported on both sides on slender marble pillars, whose marble had turned yellow – from sunlight or from age? – and whose crowns were in the Roman style. Between the ancient wood and the marble there was both a balance and a rustic incongruity, the peasant rhythm of which was exaggerated by the curve of the wooden balcony that surrounded the nave of the church and that was interrupted at the altar; the balcony was now empty and dark, but despite that I felt that it was inhabited, that it was watching us, awake and conscious of our concerns.

The altar screen was also of brown wood that had now turned almost black, its edges missing or eaten away. It had dovetailed joints, in which the beige inlayed ivory had faded, and in some of which there were pale-coloured hollows in place of the lost ivory. In his ancient, gilded vestments, Father Andrawus's nasal voice came to us with an expansive, resounding tone, then sank into a hoarse Coptic whisper, with a pure, physical pleasure, as he served the divine presence in the altar sanctuary.

Uncle Gorgi's own chants had an echo that penetrated the vastness of the spirit, and filled the nave of the church. Despite this, his hollow voice rang out with a pure music. It was a voice that we knew for its foulness and obscenity, but now it was refined and purified, with a reverberation that was sweet and commanding at the same time.

Then I felt the earth spinning.

Uncle Gorgi was hanging aloft, motionless, firmly attached to the church dome.

On one side of the dome, up there, fixed without a sound or a word, with his huge body and his galabiya covered by the sash of a senior deacon, though its colour was no longer bright red but was now a dull grey.

I did not believe my eyes, I do not believe them, though I knew perfectly well that what I was seeing was nothing but the truth. I could see him, himself, with us below, leading the junior deacons, striking the brass triangle and echoing cymbals as he chanted in that voice of his that was full of sanctity and earthiness at the same time, in his galabiya encircled with the bright red sash.

First of the divine reciters, leader of hundreds, head of the angels, wielder of the sharp, fiery sword. Gorgi had seen him, Gorgi who did not see.

I see him now in his earthly form and no one else?

While Gorgi was raised up.

The adulterous sinner, then, has no place in the sanctuaries dedicated to the Lord with his stern love.

I was stifling in the earth of Tarrana, drunk on its heat and frenzied raptures.

How I needed a strong will, a tyrannical and mocking will, even!

That could have saved me from the death of empty mornings, from hours of continuous death between fading erotic dreams. Fantasies that hissed Hamida, Heneina, Linda, Rahma, concubines and slave girls, temptresses of *The Thousand and One Nights*, dark-eyed virgins, singing-girls, boyish houris of the meadows, immature incarnations and hot fantasies, lolling, yawning horrors with sharp teeth, mermaids and insatiable genies of the Nile, as if it were for me to gather up the ruins of these creatures that could not be repaired. I wanted to make for myself new, virgin goddesses, half-baked intentions, fits of anger, sterile extensions, salty swamps on which to open the courtyard of my breast, whose brackish surface is covered by unpleasant watermoss, the fruits of a troubled spirit that is not of the spirit. That day will never come when the stranger returns to his sanctuary; he will not return to his homeland, no homeland come to him, where is his land on the thighs of his wife in the grave of his goddess he has no land, love is the first fruit of the soul.

Dreams and ideas, foolish and commonplace, ignorant, even, twisted and spun.

Love is a surrender beyond all intellect and all understanding. Ha, ha!

The first time I saw him, he had stretched out his hand to me, by force of habit, for me to kiss it.

I can see this youth, small and thin, in his thirteenth year, pulling hard on the priest's hand without bending down to give it the customary respectful kiss, as he looked him straight in the eye. The priest looked at him in astonishment for a moment, then said: 'Are you Sawirus's daughter's boy? By the name of the cross and the sign of the cross, may your guardian neither slumber nor sleep.' He gave a good-natured and tolerant laugh that seemed to come from the bottom of his chest and I loved him a lot after that, although I never kissed his hand.

He liked to come to play cards (Basra, he never changed the game) or backgammon or dominoes with Grandfather Sawirus or Grandmother Amalia (who could play dominoes extremely well), or even with my young aunt Sarah. Aunt Wadida, however, didn't like games. He always ended up losing (can you believe it?), but would be happy and relaxed nonetheless. He would take off his round blue turban, put it on the pillow laid out on the mastaba in front of the main door and play with great enthusiasm. He saw nothing to stop him cheating occasionally as he played, openly but unsuccessfully, as if he wanted to give himself away, and when someone caught him he would laugh from the bottom of his heart. He loved Grandmother Amalia's food. 'What are you making for lunch today, Umm Yunan? No, no, your mulukhiyya is pure honey! God keep your hands safe and preserve your power!'

Gorgi the deacon would sometimes come and join in the game. He was a skilful player, with practised and sensitive fingers, a little bent from excess flesh. He would feel the dominoes quickly between his thumb and index finger and knew the numbers from the small, round hollows on the face of the domino. But despite Mu'allim Gorgi's considerable skill, acknowledged in every household, he would always be beaten by Father Arsanius, my grandfather Sawirus and Abu Fanus's cousin. 'Hey, do you always want to win everything, Gorgi, my brother?', he would tease him at the end of every game. And the deacon would give a great belching laugh and lick his dark, shining lips with his tongue, remembering the sweet taste of other pleasures and wins that had nothing to do with figures. He would carry on laughing as his round paunch quivered in his silk summer caftan. 'God make things turn out for the best, my children!'

Father Andrawus would come after noon in his black silk gown – I only knew Tarrana in summer – over a snow-white galabiya with a closed collar, starched but soft, even when the temperature was at its height.

I never saw his wife. Their little house was at the south end of the village, next to the church. She never came to visit us. I heard from the grown-ups that she never left the house, but many years later I learned that she had finally left it for Bobello and that Father Andrawus had quickly joined her.

Only a few people came to uncle Gorgi and Sitt Hunayna Mu'awwad's wedding, celebrated in a church that on that day seemed particularly wide and spacious, and empty. Despite the fact that we were there, the women of Tarrana did not come, as if they had made an agreement in advance. Father Andrawus dealt with his sacristan and senior deacon's wedding at a brisk pace, as if he just wanted to make a quick escape from a slightly embarrassing affair, despite the fact that Jesus was the Lord of forgiveness and never refused the repentance of those who knocked on his door. My uncle Gorgi and his brother Basili went out (Basili carried on the shoulders of some young lads, his body shaking uncontrollably) from the mudbrick chamber in the nave of the church to the house built by Misak Banhawi, God rest his soul, beside the old waterwheel on the outskirts of the village.

At the end of this summer Aunt Rosa and Aunt Salome were visiting them in this house, at the north end of the village, with Linda, Rahma and Khadra, and I, too, went with them.

I was greeted by Sitt Hunayna Mu'awwad with a pale, drooping hand with not a sinew in it, like a sticky sweet, and a whiff of the odour of Sudanese sandalwood. She was reclining, half-lying, half-sitting, on an Ottoman-style sofa in an inner room that was warm, despite the door and window being open.

Her plump body oozed and trickled from her black silk peasant gown decorated with large red flowers that were linked by green, interlocked branches, the threads of the branches rising and falling with the hidden breezes of the body. Her breast moved up and down with her warm breath, filling the upper part of her dress, and the rounded contours of her cleavage behind it were magnificent and arousing. Her eyes gleamed, painted with kohl in a thick, dark blue line, so dark that it was almost black, and the whites of her slightly swollen eyeballs were clear and bright.

I asked Father Andrawus what he would do with the sacred books, with the religious picture torn when the ruins of the church's south wall collapsed on it, and with the smashed icons. He answered that he would burn them, of course, and throw the ashes remaining from them into the flowing waters of the Nile, or bury them in consecrated ground in Bobello, so that they would not be trampled under foot or desecrated.

He said: 'These are holy things, my child; they deserve our total reverence. How can we let them be defiled, or treated with contempt? Even to insult them is evil, a dangerous evil; who knows what the consequences may be for us as individuals or for the whole village? These are matters for excommunication, excommunication, my child.'

OK, I asked him, what was he going to do about the collapsed south wall? When would he repair or rebuild it? Would it cost a lot? He said that it wasn't a matter of cost, but rather a matter of the Imperial Decree. 'What?' I asked him. 'It's a long story, my child,' he replied. 'If a church suffers any damage or collapses, then a royal command must be issued from the palace, signed by his Majesty the Sultan and published in the official gazette, and it can only be acted on from the date of its publication. This is something that goes back a long way, to 1856, around a hundred years ago, that is, or ninety rather, a little less than ninety.' I recalled that Father Andrawus despite everything was a good priest who had studied his lessons well. He said that it was called the Sublime Edict, that it was written in fancy characters called Khatt Humayuni, and that it stipulated that a request had to be submitted to the Sublime Porte for the building or repair of any churches, though the royal palace had now taken the place of the Sublime Porte. Even after the British occupation, the abolition of the Ottoman caliphate and the end of Egypt's status under the Sultan, even after independence and 26 February, after Sa'd Zaghlul and the constitution, Nahhas Pasha, Makram 'Ubayd and the declaration of war, he had actually written to the bishop of Beheira, he said, and the bishop would do what was necessary. The bishop was essential, and he, Father Andrawus, could do nothing.

When we left Tarrana three years later, the south wall was still in a state of collapse.

After the revolution, the setback of 1967, the 1973 crossing of the Suez Canal, the economic open-door policy, the awakening, and the end of the twentieth century imminent, the decree is still in force. Is the south wall still in a state of collapse?

Father Andrawus knew all the tricks. He left the tent fabric taut and built an improvised wall of mud brick one night to block up the gap that was open to daylight and the light of the heavens. He built it secretly, without the knowledge of the authorities. The authorities in the district capital and in Cairo, that is. As for the 'umda and the shaykh al-balad, as for anyone who mattered, in fact, they knew but kept quiet.

Shaykh Hamid al-Dasuqi, God bless him, – you know him, with his upright bearing and eyes like a hawk – Shaykh Hamid said to the watchman, 'Uways Abu al-Mu'ati, who was standing open-mouthed in front of him, 'God damn you, man'. Then he sprang up and shouted at him to keep his mouth shut. 'Cut it out,' he said. 'That's quite enough of this. Is it a disease with you all, or what? You should be ashamed of yourself. Just pretend not to notice and keep quiet!'

As for our 'umda, our good, compliant, corpulent 'umda who loved peace and quiet, it was as if he had heard and seen nothing. He did not speak.

The stones on the heap of rubble were left in their place. The children (and grown-ups), simply by walking over the rubble, flattened a narrow path across it as they crossed the blind alley. I once saw Hamida the leper clinging to the stones with the stumps of her wasted fingers, covering them with the edge of her veil and holding on to the edges of the stones as she clambered across the marble of ruins smooth from the passage of feet. I saw her losing her balance completely on the way down and thought I heard her groaning, mewing, uttering a stifled complaint.

You who hurl the spear from your eyes unclouded in the twisting lane in which is a single rock and the remnants of a cat many days dead fertile days deprived for ever of fruit setting sail for the north on the surface of tranquil waters are you the fish or the fisherman are you the hidden genie or the carrier of firewood and sorrows wandering naked under your single torn patched garment brought down by the warmth of the khamasin to your body risen from the dead pelted with fine sand clothed in hollows and the fruit of ravines and stones of the hills like an ancient Coptic chant my black swan killed by a houri stories and tales under the light of a corn cob with torn edges its wick drowned in warm oil the nymph of the Nile is loved the music of radiance will the light ever make amends to you will it take from you the weight of your sin in which is no fault but is rather purity and innocence together you dance the dance of the dervishes in their trance the dance of the butterflies of the field the dance of the goose slain under the palm tree in the courtyard of Sitt Amalia you dance without sound to the rhythm of the flood as it surges and snarls.

The smell of the water in the twilight pool covering the threshing floor has a slight whiff of decay and a hidden fertility, with little waves of nostalgia glittering on its surface. Suddenly the ravens croak, coming in a flock in successive waves from the direction of the sant and sycamore trees on the dusty Nile embankment that is now deserted.

When I got out of the Peugeot taxi, the embankment, now level and black with asphalt, was crowded with cars – Mercedes, Volvos and Nasrs – and goods lorries loaded with baked bricks, bags of cement and cartons of pesticide. I found no trace of the big old house. In its place, some three-storeyed concrete houses had been built. My heart would not let me enter the church. Its walls seemed threadbare; the water had soaked into them, leaving dark, crooked lines on them. I did not go to Bobello. Aunt Wadida, now aged, was all welcoming in her peasant dialect and rustic expressions ready for every occasion, and had made me lunch of fried eggs and sour cheese. I had arrived unexpectedly and without warning. Uncle Fanus looked at me with narrowed, screwed up eyes, pale now from old age, and said, 'Can this be right, sir? Why didn't you tell us ? We would have come to meet you at the station. Did you come by taxi? Goodness, I am cross with you. You should have said, but here's something to eat, anyway – a friend's onion is worth a lamb, isn't it? … Welcome!' He didn't eat with me, having lunched earlier that morning. 'It's a long time, a long time, sir! Sa'diyya has married, and 'Aisha is with her cousin, Ibn Barsum, you remember him, in Kafr al-Dawwar. Unsiyya, come on, say hallo to your cousin! The children, you know, one's in the army and two abroad, may God preserve them and bring them back safely.'

I saw no smoke from ovens or fires rising into the air to be filtered by the trees. My uncle Fanus complained to me, saying that agriculture had been hit and that it was a dying profession. A skilled peasant's daily wage was now virtually worthless. I heard the hum of televisions and videos until it was nearly dawn. The tall new lamp-posts stayed lit throughout the night until late morning the next day, casting their circles of light on groups of people sitting cross-legged on the ground – groups of men and youths returning from Iraq, Libya or Kuwait – waking up from a deep sleep, rubbing their bleary eyes. Their heads were shaven, empty of everything except for images of films of raw, gushing emotions, blurred memories of karate kicks and cowboy fights, and the contortions of male and female bodies, plastic, artificial bodies that slithered and groped in glossy porno couplings, their streamlined antics devoid of any eroticism, indeed of any real obscenity, so perfect and polished were they. I did not see any women going down to the Nile to draw water or wash clothes. We now had piped running water. The women didn't kill the fatted calf at home, it was now frozen meat and chickens from the co-op, with the mechanised bakery open for two or three hours every day. As for those who had missed the boat and fallen on hard times, they retreated to the ruins of their old, tumbledown houses with melancholy hearts.

But the crows still bring me the unleavened bread of desire, I said, the crows are Noah's messengers that did not return, the children of Christ, the candles standing burning under the fluttering of their black wings under the lofty dome fighting their smallness, their uncertain flame and their emaciated bodies, flying gently, their heart a wick that knows it must go to be burnt and does not care, it has no pride in itself, even though its pride is inextinguishable, raising its light heroically to a dark heaven on the threshold of the castle inhabited by the beloved Lord, God, neither male nor female, in the East of the Holy of Holies, my citadel is empty now, its wall collapsed, deserted by the beloved (she who said she was beloved), the candles' wax now spent.

Dark, with no light for myself in myself?
You are a need for the heart
Unsatisfied and unsatisfying
A need
Unending.

6
The Icon

Father Andrawus had been able to rescue an old icon from among the ruins of the collapsed south wall of the church, he said.

His hands refused to throw it into the heart of the fire that he had lit himself in the dusty courtyard of the church from clean, stripped cotton stalks and branches from the broad Christ's thorn tree that shaded the church and stretched over the wall of the big house. The village children had cut them for him and left them to dry and harden, so that the fresh leaves lost their moisture, rustling with a sound that grated on the nerves. He said to me: 'I have seen to it myself that there is not a single piece of dung in this fire, no newspaper pages or anything unclean.'

Into the fire he threw the old coloured cardboard pictures with their broken frames and faded look, and copies of the Gospels that could no longer be read. Their pages had been destroyed by falling objects – stones, the heavy marble column, and the wood of the old cupboard inlaid with ivory (what a disaster!) of which only fragments and splinters now remained. But he saved the books of chants stamped with the picture of the great patriarch Kyrolles the fifth, the reformer, and a valuable copy of the Book of Martyrs, and the icon.

'Come to the church tomorrow, at four o'clock, after Mass,' he said. 'There are some bits still almost intact. The other bits have gone. Come and see them. Take anything you like. Damaged, yes, but there are still useful things there.'

I took, from among the ruins, a few loose sections of the History of the Coptic Nation and Church, by the Englishwoman, Mrs A. L. Pitcher, on the first page of which I read that the price of the complete four volumes was 40 piastres, and that it had been printed at the expense of the owner of the Misr newspaper in 1900 AD, corresponding to 1616 by the Coptic calendar. Also, some pages of The Ceremony of Holy Matrimony According to the Rite of the Orthodox Coptic Church of St Mark, published at the expense of the archpriest Philothaus al-Maqari at the Saint Makarios Press, Old Cairo; and half of a book called The Shining Pearl in the Spiritual Chants and Hymns of Praise Sung in the Churches of the Coptic Patriarchate, 8th edition, 1637 AM, corresponding to the year 7413 of the Creation, 1913 of the Incarnation according to the Eastern Christian calendar used by the Copts and Ethiopians, 1921 AD according to the Western Christian calendar, and. 1339 AH by the Islamic reckoning. For this page alone, I was pleased to take the half of the book that was left after the stone falls had ripped it apart.

I left Father Andrawus carefully gathering up the ashes of his fire on a new earthenware plate with a rough surface, whose pores were still open and raw coloured. The running water would carry them away.

Uncle Gorgi, the church precentor, was standing at the door, without going in. When he recognised my footsteps, he said to me: 'Good evening, Sir! Take your time! Watch out that you don't slip like your uncle Gorgi Always take your time!'

'The bliss of a headstrong impulse with no dilly-dallying!', I said to myself.

My imagination had been fired by Uncle Gorgi's visits, at once secret and well publicised, to Sitt Heneina.

The blind lyre player who takes his place on the left of the temple.

The thief on his left.

He took off his tarboosh, showing the strong, rough, curly hair on his head. He wrapped his neck in a garland of fresh basil and wild thyme.

He strikes the bronze triangle and cymbals the din of the music and the wailing of Golgotha in the holy sanctuary the chanting of the wise monkey the mating of the cow Hathor under the great Christ's thorn tree the great bull jumps once then falls off her then again the boys and men gather the bull is tethered with a long loose rope under its horns there is tied a strip of rough coloured cloth on which is a lotus with pale soft leaves its wild flower erect lust of hands alone two eyes nothing but the thrust of the huge body fiery and fierce surrounding a welcoming dough-like feminine mass that eludes one's grasp a massive female sinking under the pouncing legs the exhausted harp sounds out its jubilations with its unending strings of glory taut and broken taking to its bosom the weak and crippled and sick not out of pity for it has no pity but rather from the heat of lust and the impatience of seduction, gratification and satisfaction. In the darkness of lovemaking of which I was a part I seemed to hear the groans of love, the moans of love, 'Ah! be careful, man!', and the bottomless depths, 'Oh, what a cheek! What a nerve you've got! Don't play games with me, woman!', as he seeks the passageway of love into her welcoming, frightening body, inflamed by the fires of lust and fulfilment, and they fall together into the pit.

As if it was said:

Do not let your heart wither

Follow nothing but the promptings of your passion

Put garlands of water lilies on your head

Wrap your sister's neck in the flowers of the lily

Before you reach – inevitably – the shore of silence.

In the darkness that had fallen on the wide, empty nave, in the cloudy, murky afternoon, I entered.

The nave of the church was deserted.

It was barely lit by the few candles burning silently under the ivory-coloured, marble pillars. It occurred to me that they had been taken from the Temple of Bobello, ages ago possibly.

The smell of the burning candles, the feeling of awe in this surprising emptiness that seemed to me primitive, wooden, propped up by old marble.

In the silence around me, I thought I heard a stifled whisper, whose source I could not discern, like a hidden lament from a blocked-up tomb, a man's hopeless, defeated sobbing, the sound of a soul that had found no rest or comfort. Or so I thought.

'Why, Lord? Why? Never in my life have I denied Your Gospel, Oh Lord of glory! Never in my life have I polluted water in the river, in the canal, or in the irrigation channels, large or small. Never in my life have I kept milk from the mouth of a creature suckling, be it boy-child or calf, or even a girl from a man's loins and a woman's belly. Never in my life have I ever stopped the flow of running water. Never have I turned anyone away from the fire of the stove, or the blaze of the oven, either by night or by day. Never in my life have I ever treated anyone harshly, whether Christian or Muslim; never in my life have I snuffed out a lighted candle, Lord; never in my life have I cut a crop in season by force from the land of a neighbour or enemy; never in my life have I harboured evil in my heart, Lord. Well, why then? Why? Why do you break my heart? Why?'

I saw the icon that Father Andrawus said he had retrieved from the stones of the ruins. He said that its glass had fallen from it, all at once, as if a strong, firm hand had pulled it off by its clear, sharp edges, he said.

I saw the face of Christ, dark, with closed eyes, wrinkles across the ages sunk in the surface of the dark, wooden icon, while over its black, oily surface the glimmer of little candles danced, their lights quivering under it, while a vaguely outlined crown of thorns encircled a head tormented by unendurable burdens.

Jesus was weeping, dry, arid tears, unabating. Almost without tears, without sound.

He raised his head. His face in the broken icon gazed at his other face in front of him, kneeling on the church's bare tiled floor. He had wrapped his head in a dusty headdress, dark and prickly to the touch, his galabiya falling over his bony shoulders, his body tense under the old cloth. Even though he knelt, he was still erect, as if he were still being crucified, no surrender or abandonment in him. Even amidst this sobbing that rose slowly, without bursting forth, from a hidden layer under the earth, from the pain and agony of misery, the tears of Jesus, not in his glory but in his earthly torment, fell from the icon, drop by drop, onto the floor of the church.

I saw his outstretched hand, marked by the green, leafy cross, his hand pierced with the marks of the great nails stretching out in compassion and dignity as he placed it on the head raised up to him. The dark face was dry and furrowed, contracted with sufferings that no one would ever know.

The age-old peasant of Tarrana, the Copt whom the world had forgotten, struck down by the unremitting advance of time. Not a counterpart but a reincarnation. The head was wrapped in a skullcap, with a dark shawl over it. From it furrows of toil and the heart's sorrows descended, like black crevices. The icon saved from among the ruins.

Inside myself I hummed softly and boiled over with anger.

Not from faith. Not from piety.

Would this icon stay buried, throbbing with pain, split apart, humbled yet unconquered? Or would it disappear and fade away, with only the fabric of the black wood remaining, as if disowned? Would that man be sanctified who stretched out to it a hand with bruised bones, a hand dripping great round drops of blood, one after the other, with a muffled ring on the bare floor, drop after drop?

Would he be filled with life and blessings, or would he be struck down by drought and deafness?

Would we hear with him the life-giving word? What was it? Or would we be seized by blindness before his gospel, painted in *tempera* by a hand that better knew how to break up the ground with a hoe than to mix egg-yolk with the ecstasy of a drunken heart?

No, the slight but stubborn body, unendingly repeated on this earth on which are repeated glad tidings, one after the other, life-giving without end and without fulfilment.

The melodies of the harp, the song of the flute, the clash of the cymbals, the chanting of the *dhikr*, the wine of the dervishes, the squeaking of delicate carvings, the rustle of boxes of Savo, Rabso and hand soap, the blare of TV ads, hurtful and foul with their flickering current, orchestra chairs around the continuous convulsions of a belly dancer tied up in nylon lamp cords, thin red and green phosphorus and fluorescent tubes reflected on still waters in swimming pools sterilised with chlorine, stones from modern times also fall, in an incoherent and shamefully coded language, the knocking of wood, the cries of young girls drunk out of their minds, the beating of drums and the call of the curlew endlessly echoing in the poured out light of the half-bright, half-dusky moon. All theologies, all ideologies, piercing parrot cries, the lushness of wild plants, monstrous prickly pears with outstretched branches, octopuses with tentacles eager to embrace and kill in the arms of an unsullied love, the button at the centre of a belly soft and dough-like in colour and to touch, a swimming fish, a gold, piercing eye spilled out without closing, rusty iron staircases with their electricity cut off by which you descend to the navel of Ramleh underground station, the smells of tomatoes, okra and swollen green peppers, a slightly rotten fake testicle, discharge of flesh, frozen limbs that convict you with no right of appeal, from hooks with triangular teeth that sink into the flesh of the sea, on their sides spring forth small red flowers, bright, delicate and fragile, on which is the dew of blood and round teardrops on the two small domes of the breasts and the large dome of the belly the faces of the icons the faces of the prisoners of Turah and Abu Za'bal, the interrogation vaults and cellars of Caracalla, the dark pit under the ground in Fez, Damascus, Toledo, Granada, Sanaa, Jerusalem reeking with the stench of the body suspended by its hands and feet with iron hooks, with the odour of urine and pungent smell of hard, piled up human stools, on which new excrement was dropping, the chains only unfastened to open the grave with no memorial no name no tombstones the opening sura of the Fatiha of the Book from merciful hearts and our Father who art in heaven mumbled for fear that it should be heard by the red cardinals and a thousand thousand faces struck from the depths of time to the infinities of the horizon piled up in the same proportion black with grey lines on them and open eyes murdered without a word without a witness the wide asphalt roads clean and black driven over by Mercedes, Volvos and Nasr Fiats surrounded by a breeze of exhaust fumes that quickly pass, a thousand thousand thousand superimposed faces from which all glory all crowns of thorns have fallen, sacks of camphorous manure packed tightly on both sides of a hairless, spotted grey donkey, coming from the ancient Apollo ready to pounce on shame and toil and the torment of untiring lust for every she-donkey that lies in the field or passes on the road.

Chasing dreams, tilting at windmills.

* * *

Grandfather Sawiris, realising that the tin of tobacco was empty, sent me to bring him a new one from Shenuda the grocer, just as he used to, even at night, when we lived at the house in number 12 Street in Gheit el-'Inab. It was after the call to evening prayer, and Father Andrawus, Uncle Gorgi and Uncle Selwanes had all gone home. 'Come on, quickly,' my grandfather said to me, 'or he'll shut up the shop.' I knew how gloomy the alleyways of Tarrana were at night, pitch black in fact, and my heart trembled with anxiety. 'Pull yourself together, lad! Shame on you!' I said to myself. But the night was dark, pitch black, the moon invisible, even the sky seemed blocked, and the pinpricks of the stars were ineffective. The walls of the houses were low, dark and menacing, all closed up, showing not a chink of light.

I felt my way with my feet over the surface of the narrow alley that twisted back on itself, careful not to step into any soft dung or bang into a hard mound of earth. I stretched my hands out in front of me and to my sides, seeking support from the blank walls. The road had no end, no conclusion.

I felt warm breaths beside me.

I recognised them.

A bodily presence, a warm sigh, I could almost see it in the total darkness.

Hamida the leper.

It was she, she, I had not a shadow of doubt.

But she had died, disappeared, vanished.

Had she not died?

Mu'allim Shenuda had seen her himself, he had sworn to it. He had seen her floating on the waters of the Nile, all swollen up, with her black veil half submerged in the water, and the current had carried her past the village.

Beside me.

Her plaintive moaning, full but subdued, submissive, pained, demanding, disturbing.

She was limping a little still, but her skin was smooth and polished.

Her lips were on my lips, soft and moist, her saliva a little sweet. Her fingers, quite firm and full of soft flesh, passed over my face gently and tenderly as she kissed me again and again, and my body was all a-tremble, as I embraced her to my love-crazed breast.

She said to me – did she say it? – in a voice that was faint, very faint, but still clear, with a hint of authority in it, and a crystal-clear tone despite its great softness, like a passionate whisper, 'My lamb, my brother!'

'Amm Shenuda said to me 'Goodness me! What's happened? Is everything all right? Is anything wrong? Your face is pale as a sheet, and you're sweating like a pig. Come here, my boy; is everything all right? Are you sure? OK, a tin of tobacco for your grandfather Sawiris? Right you are, sir. On account? Anything you say. At your service, sir, and at Father Sawiris's service! Give him my best greetings and tell him to start rattling his pockets. I'm coming to play backgammon, and I shan't be leaving him alone!'

I said to myself, 'He who said he was alone in the gloom of the darkness while bearing the burden of a love whose weight he could not feel, he is now in the light.'

I said to myself, 'I wish it were so!'

I said to Father Andrawus, 'Why didn't you let his wife go into the church to pray with him? He was very sad, very lonely.'

She had no name.

He said, 'Because she had given birth to that daughter of theirs who died seven days after she was born.'

I said: 'The hawk that swoops on the old tower every time, time after time, snatches the daughter of the bright vessel plunging into the night.'

He said, 'Because she had not purified herself from the blood of childbirth, and the Bible says, "She shall not come to the sacred place until she has completed the days of her purification. If she gives birth to a female child she shall be unclean for two weeks, and for a further sixty-six days shall remain impure in her blood, and shall only enter afterwards, after eighty days and nights". Only after that will I deliver over her head the prayer of absolution, "We ask and beseech you, lover of mankind, that you should incline to your servant, that your spirit of holiness may be restored within her. Grant absolution to her, who has come seeking to enter into the place of Your holiness." Even our Mother, the Virgin Mary, who conceived without spot of sin and bore the Messiah without impurity from a door that had not been breached, even she, the Virgin, did not enter the sanctuary until forty days had passed, to be worthy of the holy communion of mysteries.'

I asked, 'Why only forty days? Because it was Jesus?'

'No,' he replied angrily, 'because Jesus was male. For a female child it is after eighty days, for a male child forty days only. The punishment of the female sex; didn't she eat of the apple before Adam? She led him on to the original temptation. Did not the Lord say to her: "With pain shall you give birth. To your husband will your desires submit, and he will rule over you."?'

Who gathered the wind in his hands? Who wrapped the waters in a cloak?

Everything is forgotten and passes. Why this chasing of dreams and pursuit of fantasies? Why, all right, should I light candles that will die? And light them in my heart? Or so he said.

Why, all right, should I try to sing in the face of the wind when I have no voice, why did I write in the sand on the island, beside the plantation of melons that were not yet ripe? 'Beauty is a deception', I said. 'Beauty is false,' I said, but I did not believe it for a single moment. The tears of the oppressed flow away with the rivers, of no importance whatever. The cup of joy disappears in foam that is light in the sun. Towers and castles are dust unto dust, and the hearts of the prophets are buried under the follies of the world. Why the desolation of the soul, why death? They said, 'A city destroyed without walls, a man with no power over his own soul.' My soul is power. My body is power. My love, my lust, my longing for the impossible are lines on the sand on the shore. Impossible love, impossible justice. But I do not tire, I never tire, of drawing line after line. It is not that I yearn for lips that are like a wire of crimson, or eyes like doves. Beauty is my feast and I am ravenous. The wounds of love are faithful, true, but there is no cure for them, they cannot be stitched. Have mercy on those that toss on the bed; is mercy the revolt of the wise or is it folly and weakness? Do you hear the plaintive moans? What does it matter? Are you not tired of the death of the soul, of the sterile confession?

Sounds of wailing strike the walls of time and hide the sun from mankind, elegies over a cloth of sorrow on which are served a thousand bowls of black lentils, clarified lentils, salted food, pickled food, fresh milk and bees' honey, bread and pancakes made from fenugreek and barley turned grey amid the tears and singing and seeking of forgiveness for the great sin through the sacrifice of geese, ducks and chickens, generosity to the poor and to children, entering the wine tent, yearning for a sight of the door, pouring melted sugar, pouring caster sugar, throwing sweets, planting walnuts and almonds, spreading delicious shelled peanuts over the 'Ashura porridge, the jackal raising his head to the full moon and howling to Thoth, the messenger of the gods, the bearer of the preserved tablet on the day of knowledge, the day when Adam and Eve met each other and saw that they were naked, the day when

87

Noah left his great ark after his message from the crows, the day the lovers' imam was martyred.

When, a long time later (or so it seemed), I emerged from the detention camps, I learned that my grandfather Sawiris had died in Tarrana and been buried in Bobello. I hadn't seen him for years. I had almost forgotten his ancient face, tanned and wizened by the suns of numberless days as he patiently watched his fishhooks by the salt lake in Alexandria or the Tarrana canal.

His days of glory had long passed and he had returned to Tarrana, a broken man. Had he also been broken by Aunt Sarah's marriage to a worker in the spinning factory in Karmuz by the name of Gorgis Rizq? I did not attend the wedding myself and was scarcely aware of it, but I had heard that Gorgis was addicted to hashish. When Aunt Sarah objected to the hashish parties in their one room in Ghabriyal, he dealt her a single blow with a pitcher and made a gash in her head She went to the government hospital and filed a complaint about him, then fled for protection to the house of her younger brother, Uncle Suryal. Gorgis tried to make up to her and seek her forgiveness, weeping real tears, so she went back to him but he beat her again and again, whenever she upset him – as indeed, she was very good at doing. There was no doubt that he loved her very much, in his own way. That was why he beat her and hurt her so badly every time. The church intervened and extracted from him an undertaking through the good offices of the priest but he continued to beat her, alternately furious and repentant, until he died, at quite a young age, after having three girls and one boy by her.

After the death of Gorgis Rizq, Aunt Sarah travelled to Asyut, having discovered the faith of the Protestant Missionaries and the Evangelical Church. It was as if she had washed her hands of Orthodoxy altogether. The Protestants appealed to her, won her over, took her children into their schools and gave her support. So she came to know God's service and learned by heart the Bible and the mumbo-jumbo of conversion and comfort in the Lord. So now she was a preacher and an evangelist, wandering the land from Port Said to Aswan in a black dress, travelling with nothing but the Bible in her hand, and a handbag with a second black dress and a single change of clothes. She no longer wore anything but black, with no ornaments except for a leather necklace with a large wooden cross on the end of it, not so much an ornament as a proclamation. Christ would speak to her and call her to travel to Damietta or Qus or Minuf, where she knew no one, and she would travel at once, by train, bus or shared taxi. She would enquire about the local Christians, go into their homes, preach to them, speak to them of the Bible and spend the night in one of their houses. And she would not hesitate to tell the head of the household or any of his family off if they smoked a cigarette or turned on the television. She lived the life of the prophets and did their works.

Then our Lord began to call her to go to Beirut, Baghdad, and Amman. She did not hesitate for a moment. She would arrange the price of the air ticket, then go, with nothing but her famous handbag and the Bible. I asked her once, later, 'But Aunt Sarah, does He come to you in a dream and speak to you?'

She replied, 'No! When I am awake. He speaks to me as you are speaking to me now. I know His voice. Praise be to God, Satan tries me also, and speaks to me with the voice of Jesus, but I know him at once, and I forsake him without a thought.'

Amidst the hardships of the sea of life that she had plunged into with such calmness of spirit despite the clashing of the waves, her three grown-up daughters died after they had grown up. Two of them had married and left her grandchildren with the Protestants. Her youngest child, Rumani, emigrated and eventually settled in Brazil. He was of small build, all vitality, and his eyes were full of dreams; he wrote me two or three postcards and visited me recently, telling me stories about vast farms and *haciendas* that he rode through on the backs of thoroughbred horses, and about bloody vendettas between himself and old-established, landowning families in which shots were fired, poisons prepared and poured into cups, jinns employed and evil spirits summoned. But he overcame all the conspiracies. He said this in the tone of someone relating fleeting, everyday daily events, in the same voice that he used to tell me how he had bought pineapples from the supermarket in Rio de Janeiro for the equivalent of 5 piastres or less, or that he had taken a taxi to the estate of a man whose daughter was in love with him (Rumani, that is) and who was opposing her family and her fiancé's family for his sake, foiling the demons who surrounded him in his sleep. He was very persuasive and very straightforward as he told me all this, for he believed in it and knew many tricks of black magic. But all these were recent events. Grandfather Sawiris, whom Rumani never saw, died before Gorgis Rizq, the husband of his favourite daughter. Had his heart been broken because he had refused to marry her to Fanus, the only man who had ever loved her? Until the moment of his death, however, he held himself erect, looking up and never lowering his eyes for anyone, or so Uncle Fanus told me. In the midst of all my troubles, as I tried to scrape a living and stood bewitched before the yearnings of love and absolute despair, I scarcely paid the news of his death any attention.

Now with my own eyes I see again the icon of Joseph the carpenter (or is it Saint Mark or some ancient patriarch?), rescued from the rubble by Father Andrawus, or borne by two soaring angels hovering within my body, from among the piles of collapsed stones. The features of the aged face had turned black, the face from whose darkness my spirit still sought light, in the heart of its oval frame with its old wood eaten away by woodworm and hollowed out by time, split open with fine, sunken lines zigzagging its surface. On the ground, beside the gap that had been opened in the south wall, on which fell a blinding light from an everlasting day that had no evening. Cracks in the naked body, crushed by sufferings of no importance.

My mother told me that after his death, while I was in prison in Sinai, she went to Tarrana on halfway day (halfway through the great fast, that is, as she explained to me) to visit his grave.

When they arrived at Bobello, the peasant girl who worked in Sitt Amalia's house began to distribute mercy and light, in the shape of dry biscuits and dates from Nubia, to the peasant children and blind people of Tarrana, Muslims and Christians alike. A leper girl slipped among them, silent and submissive, and the peasant girl gave her a piece of warm pitta bread baked at dawn, and a handful of dates, more than she gave to the others. 'Do you remember Hamida the leper?' my mother asked me when we met later.

My grandfather Sawiris was standing. With him was his stick with the crooked handle, made from polished walnut wood, at the head of his tomb built from red brick covered in whitewash. It had a small dome, so my mother said, and his face was calm as he looked at them with a sort of pitying seriousness. Sitt Amalia hurried towards him, anxiously, perhaps wanting to clasp him to herself one last time. Perhaps. My mother said that they all heard him say clearly, in ringing tones, 'Stay where you are, Umm Yunan. Don't follow me down. It's not yet time, Amalia, it's not yet time!'

Then he was gone…

The one icon, repeated. A visible Gospel, whose sufferings were a sun in eclipse, over which darkness descended, then withdrew, then covered it again. Its light was absolute, I reject it.

Cracks in the naked wood, cracks in the body, crushed and sunken in misery. I was tired of wandering on the earth and in the evening. Where would it all end?

A continuous wandering in the regions of dream and nostalgia, through the deep chasms and barren uplands of the world within?

Or would my feet become bogged down in the murky floodwaters of my heart?

The icon quivered silently, dimly visible to me above a single candle, its ancient face marked by a black spot from a fire long ago, and lined with wrinkles. It had now turned pale and shone with love. Saint Elizabeth, mother of John, Sitt Amalia, mother of Yunan; how often have I found in her withered breast a special love that I have not found in the breast of any other woman?

Would this young child, this youth, this old man, torn in body and spirit even today, ever forget the small, round loaf of pitta bread just emerging from the oven, the inviting fragrance and delicious, penetrating smell of flour made from durra and fenugreek, sprinkled with fine, black caraway seeds, as she spread the soft, seed-flecked face of the loaf for him with a fresh, full layer of butter, which melted and seeped into the bread so that it glistened – for its taste and smell can still be savoured to this day? Would he ever forget her narrow waist – the warmest and softest that he had ever found? When he could not hold back his tears, she alone would pat him on the head gently, silently, with her firm but tender hand. Would he ever forget her prayers? 'May He keep you safe at every step and make his creatures love you, my grandchild, may Jesus bless you and the Virgin protect you on every path.' Would he ever forget how with the sternness and strength of love she ruled the house in Gheit el-'Inab that teemed with his three uncles, Yunan, Nathan and Suryal, with his uncles' wives, Esther and Maria, with his aunts Wadida and Sarah before their marriage, with his mother who had a wing of the house to herself with his proud but soft-hearted father? She ran the household with wisdom and authority, her word was *the* word, her orders *the* orders. Would he forget how her life ended in his aunt Hanuna's flat in 'Asafra? Her legs and arms were now paralysed, her tiny body had withered, as she crept around with her hands and feet on the floor, unable to raise herself. Uncle Maqar, the negro slave, Aunt Hanuna's husband, would wash her wasted body and brittle bones of the excrement that she could not now not control. How she looked up at him, screwed up on the ground, when he came to see her for the last time, he realised later. Although she looked at him with hollow, cloudy eyes, her ruined body still had its old pride and arrogance. At first, she did not recognise him and continued to stare at him as old people do, all her will concentrated in the effort of recognition, without success. Then all at once her dry, wrinkled face brightened, and she whispered to him, 'Jesus bless your every step, son of my daughter.' That was all. Just that. Then she left him as if she had forgotten him, and crept away slowly, dragging her body to a corner of the narrow room that was her refuge, finally, on this earth. Where was the lofty palm tree in the courtyard of the Tarrana house, surging with intimacy and with life?

The boy Barsum, Uncle Fanus's brother, told me he had heard from his father that Rosa and Salome, who were also now withered, dried out and knotted like stalks of cotton for burning, had in the days of their youth been fair as the full moon and beautiful as gazelles. 'Impossible!' I said. 'That is what they said, by God!' he said. 'There was a big story in days gone by about Father Wahba, the brother of Grandfather Sawiris. It was said that Father Wahba was seized by love for them both together, and that he couldn't settle on either one of them, or even recognise which one of them was Rosa and which Salome. In the end he started talking to himself, so it was said, then he started beating himself and pelting other people and animals with stones and bricks and shouting, 'Who am I? Who am I, my children?' 'Where did the beauty and the splendour go?' I asked. 'Does the water of life drain away, and the body dry up, just like that?' 'The girl who used to bake for them in those days,' he said, 'the girl who filled their water jars from the Nile, grazed the animals on the embankment, and cleaned the barn, so they said, was a tall, rather imposing woman, and pretty, really pretty, my boy!' When they were talking about her, he had recalled Khadra, who used to work for Aunt Rosa and Aunt Salome, and who was the spitting image of the girl they were talking about. He said that she had disappeared once, like Khadra, and that Father Wahba had beaten his head on the ground without stopping as he knelt there, then started ranting and raving, saying, 'It's my fault, I did it, no one but me ...' He said a rumour had gone around, but was then hushed up, that two men of the family had gone out by night from Father Wahba's and Grandfather Sawiris's house (they were bachelors then) and made off in the direction of Bobello. He said that there was a tomb there closed up with red baked bricks and English Portland cement. It had never been opened, and no one knew whose tomb it was.' He said, 'Those were the sort of people we were, my boy, years ago. They used to do all sorts of things, one terrible thing after another, and no one ever saw anything at all.'

I was secretly saying goodbye to Tarrana.

One day, at noon, in autumnal weather, under a sky full of light, white clouds, overcast but bright at the same time...

The Nile before the flood season had a rich, full greenness in its waters. Tufts of dark water-moss floated suspended in the slow-flowing waters, oily but agitated, teased by small whirlpools and fed by slender, surging streams.

Under the stones of the great grey house that rose abruptly from the edge of the Nile, lapped by its sluggish waters that left dark, sticky lines halfway up its walls and over which thick, twisted branches fell from sycamore, mulberry, Christ's thorn and mango trees, there was a small, emaciated, white sheep, with damp, dangling wool, being washed by some peasant children. They had taken off their short, dusty shirts and wore only baggy woollen underclothes that clung damply to their dark, slender thighs and small, quivering genitals. Their naked breasts were smooth, their chests round with sunken bones, but their faces were brimming with mischief and vitality. Their dark, handsome features had been tormented by continual but unnoticed hunger. They were shouting at one another, cursing their fathers and mothers eloquently, playfully, and noisily ...

On the wall were cotton sheets, faded woollen blankets and patched covers with stains of obvious origin. On the roofs of the closely packed mud houses, under the wing of the large house, were stacks and heaps of dung and firewood. Their walls were built of sun-dried bricks and daubed with pale, pistachio-coloured paint, under which the rough white clay seemed almost organic, alive.

A side of a broken wooden box on the ground.

A chicken coop made from thin wooden planks and palm branches, on which a white duck stood, tied up.

The thin light shone all around, absolute darkness.

7
Farah al-'Arabawi

'Uncle' Farah was no relation of mine.

Everyone used to call him 'Uncle Farah', though.

He was a nomad, who wandered in that part of the Western Desert in which we also were, near the Desert Road. He knew by heart the opening chapter of the Koran and he always said his prayers at the right time.

Tall and upright, very thin, but strong and robust nonetheless, he wore nothing but a faded white shirt that reached to a little below his knees. When he sat on the sand, you could see his round, dark knees, with their two enormous bony kneecaps. You could also catch a glimpse of his private parts hanging down, dark and enormous, still with some strength left in them apparently. Over his shoulders he had a shawl of the same pale woollen cloth, which he wrapped around his head and made into a turban; this he would unfold and set up on his knotted stick, making it into a tent and shelter under which he put his head to protect him from the noon heat as he slept, with his legs out in the sun. This heat, this absolute solitude, were his natural habitat.

How could this old bedouin, about whom in my heart I knew nothing, have stayed alive for more than half a century?

Perhaps I loved him as a thirteen-year old boy, and for that reason had got to know him.

This love has preserved him.

He used to come from some distance away, at an angle to the asphalt desert road, the 'Treaty Road',[1] as we used to call it. He would appear suddenly from behind the sand, with his slightly loping walk with its spaced-out rhythm, as if he were coming from nowhere. His bare, flat feet would bounce across the burning sand like a camel's. The soles of his feet were thick and dry. A small nail could enter them without him feeling it.

He would treat the labourers who worked with us with desert herbs and spices that he wrapped up carefully in a deep sack. He would cure the burns from hot, molten pitch, the next day, instantly stopping the throbbing pain. Cuts from nails that had penetrated a man's feet would be healed. He had ointments and powders especially to cure haemorrhoids and skin diseases. For gripes, constipation or diarrhoea, he had herbs that were steeped or boiled and left overnight in barley water. I remember that among the things he had with him were dried coriander, tamarisk leaves, galingale, onion seeds, black nightshade, safflower, blackberries, colocynths, squill, wild mint, red myrrh, mastic, tooth sticks, horse flowers, and the leaves or pith of the prickly pear, in all its different forms and shapes.

He couldn't read or write, nor did he make charms or talismans.

He would greet me with a broad smile that illuminated his dark face. His hand in mine was a living stick covered in cracked bark. For all that, it was sensitive and responsive, able to transmit a message of strange affection and love.

He would sit quite still on his knees on the sand without falling, without even tiring or shaking, in front of the big tent that Uncle Nathan and I slept in and in which we put our food and everything else – the casual labourers' headquarters, it was – near the middle of the Desert Road. He sat, relaxed and comfortable, even though there was no more than a finger's breadth, or something like that, between him and the ground. He would wrap the little bit of tobacco he had left in a thin piece of almost transparent cigarette paper, spotted with light, white stains. He would make a very thin cigarette, sticking the edge of it to the edge of his heel, then ask me for a match and amaze me, as usual, by rubbing it on his ankle as he sat there cross-legged, resting now on one foot but without touching the ground, and without losing his precarious balance for a single moment, or so it seemed to me, as he lit the match with a single scrape on the hard, dry skin, smiling a somewhat childish smile to reveal large, yellow molars, in the knowledge that he was impressing me with this unusual trick of his.

He would slowly undo the knot in the big sack hanging on

his shoulders and take out from one of the many bundles, a few handfuls of dried dates, as agreed, and I would give him a packet of Abu Ghazala tobacco in its soft, dark green paper with a clutch of cigarette papers above it, from the wooden shelf that held the stock of provisions' inside the tent.

At the beginning of the summer of 1939 my uncle said to me, 'Why don't you come with me with the seasonal workers? You'll see a bit of life and enjoy yourself, and earn yourself a few piastres at the same time!' He wrote to my father in Alexandria, who said to him, 'OK, on condition you take good care of him. An uncle is like a father, remember!' 'Take good care of him, Nathan,' Grandmother Amalia said. 'He's a darling child, and you're responsible for him, my son!' 'He's a man, mother!' my uncle replied.

Linda had stayed part of the evening with us – in Grandfather Sawiris's house, that is – until the evening call to prayer, and when she went home for the night I said goodbye with a handshake, which was not my usual practice. I usually just said 'Good evening' or '*Sa'ida*,' to which she would reply, in peasant fashion, 'And a good evening to you, my brother!' Her voice oozed charm and a hidden petulance. That night I pressed her hand a little, holding it for perhaps a second longer than usual. She gave me a heavy, silent look – not her normal look – a look of acknowledgement and secret understanding.

Rahma, on the other hand, had not waited. I never forgave her for that, and I haven't forgotten it, maybe, even now. But I wonder whether perhaps it didn't represent a deeper acknowledgement.

Aunt Wadida, Aunt Sarah and Grandmother Amalia were all awake with the morning star, when I myself woke from a disturbed and interrupted sleep. Aunt Wadida slipped some caramel drops wrapped in 'butter paper' into my pocket as she kissed me. I remembered the days at Number 12 Street in Gheit el-'Inab. Aunt Sarah kissed me artlessly on the mouth, and Grandmother Amalia clasped me in her dry, narrow bosom that reeked of oven smoke and buffalo milk. How tender was this bosom and how fragrant its embrace! Quietly, as if praying, she said, 'May your every step be safe through Jesus's blessing,' and I thought that I heard her whisper 'my love'. I was not sure I'd heard right because she had never used such an expression before, or afterwards – neither she nor my mother – as if to address someone like that was a disgrace or a weakness unforgivable for us poor Copts. I only ever heard the expression again from a woman when we were at the top of a few broad steps in our first city that lies outside space and time when, as the thin morning clouds rippled musically, she said to me: 'I am at your service, my love!' She said it in her language, in my language.

At midday, Aunt Rosa and Aunt Salome had come to the house, and said to me, almost with one voice: 'You're going to Wadi Natrun tomorrow with your uncle. We hope it goes well, son of Amalia's daughter!' And they patted me on the shoulders with wooden hands.

I said, to travel a dozen or so kilometres is still a journey, it is still to leave home.

Before the sun had even started to rise, I was on the back of a transport lorry, standing with about twenty men from Tarrana, some sharecroppers and men from the estate. Among them was 'Awad 'Awadin and his brother Hegazi 'Awadin, the husband of Khadra, whom I'd secretly said goodbye to in a romantic sense – the sort of thing that Ibrahim Nagi had in mind in his poem that starts: 'This Ka'ba that we used to walk around ...' Anyway, I returned later to my own Ka'ba after the seasonal work had finished, at the end of the summer.

Uncle Nathan sat with the driver in the cab, on the seat and floor of which were the weekly food supplies for the workers.

The lorry made its way through the desert, sometimes soft, dry, undulating sand, sometimes stony. There were no signs or landmarks between Tarrana and Khatatba to the east, and the Rest House or a bit further north, to the west, and the edges of the track through the desert were sometimes unclear. The wheels slipped on scattered sand that the wind had blown up and strewn around until they found their grip again on the track, beaten down by the wheels passing over it.

There was no landmark to be found in the dawn light that spilled out and spread slowly. When I looked back, my eyes were blinded and dazzled by the rim of the sun slowly emerging from the surface of the sand, a gold red round splinter whose circumference slowly widened, until from the edge of the horizon a fiery disk, perfectly round, slipped free.

At dawn on the Feast of Epiphany, my mother would wake

us to see the head of John the Baptist cut off by Herod's sword, passed round on the sun's blazing platter before Salome.

I felt that I was among my own family and folk.

The smell of strong, shaven heads and shaven body hair mingled with what was left of the smell of Nablus soap from yesterday's baths, with the lingering smell of women's juices, and the semen poured into them during the night – all mingled with the smell of fenugreek and maize flour in the pitta bread that quickly dried and became hard to break, unless wetted by dipping the now trembling whey (I can smell it and savour its aroma) into the black, round-bellied cooking pots covered with heaps of dry clay wrapped in scraps of women's old dresses, carefully and cunningly hidden in the bags of provisions that the young men had wrapped their knees around in the lorry as they stood, to protect them from the juddering and the ups and downs of the road.

We got down, our legs shaky from travelling in the lorry on the newly asphalted road for some kilometres after the Rest House. We had reached the gap that the workmen were supposed to level and widen, reinforcing it with sand and gravel, then covering it with tar and asphalt.

We set up the big tent at a distance of about fifty metres from the edge of the road. The Rest House sign seemed a long way away to me, but it was comforting.

A baker's wooden slab was set up for me, with a double blanket, folded twice, spread on it, and the same for Uncle Nathan. There was an improvised table made from an upturned tea chest, and a single wooden shelf – half a baker's plank set up on two rows of red clay – with the weekly rations for the labourers on it – tins of Abu Ghazala tobacco, and Coutarelli cigars in their white cardboard packets that opened upwards, like padded paper boxes, Feel cigarettes, sold singly, on a round tin plate, and little packets of tea that were only just stuck together, from the joins of which black grains of fragrant tea spilled out. In those days tea was not adulterated with coloured *molukhiya* leaves, or crushed and roasted peanuts. The sugar lumps were beside it in rectangular paper bags, arranged in rows on half a broken plate that was in turn placed at the bottom of a broken corrugated iron barrel filled with water to protect them from the ants – the most adventurous of which I would find each morning drowned in the water.

Just that. That's all.

Inside the tent there was an iron barrel full of clear, clean drinking water just for me and Uncle Nathan. A mug was fastened to it by a strong cord that passed through a hole in the curved metal wall of the barrel, under its upper edge. The barrel was covered with a square piece of wood, and its water was cool and fresh.

The other barrels outside the tent, four or five of them, were for the workmen.

Then there was always a third barrel inside the tent, beside the door – beside the opening in the cloth, that is, that was lifted by small ropes during the day, then let down and secured with strong pegs in the sand at night. This water was reserved for washing and bathing.

My job was to write out the daily wages for each worker individually – on lined paper, with a piece of carbon paper under it that I guarded with my life, for it was the only one we had. I would multiply their wages by the number of days worked, then add up the total at the end of the Friday, then write the deductions for tea, sugar and tobacco on another piece of paper, without a carbon copy – what had been taken on account, and how much it was worth – and at the end I would subtract it and hand everyone the two piastres or whatever was due to them. They stood in a disorderly queue, entering the tent one at a time, with the next person not going in until the previous one had emerged from the half raised, half lowered opening. Uncle Nathan would check my calculations and hand me the shining red piastres and millimes. The daily wage was three *ta'rifas*, and the boss got five *ta'rifas*. When we had deducted from that the allowance for tea, sugar and tobacco, then each man would get a two-piastre piece and three or four millimes at the end of Friday, with perhaps three or four piastres for the miser who economised on drinking tea or smoking, and who put up with the subsequent ridicule and mockery.

It was all of our Lord's goodness, something one should kiss one's hand for, back and palm, in gratitude.

I myself emerged at the end of Friday with a five-piastre piece, no more, no less. I saved it, and at the end of the summer I bought Plato's *Republic* in the translation by Professor Hanna Khabbaz for twenty-five piastres, and *Egyptian Civilization* by Gustave Le Bon, translated by Professor Sadiq Rustum, for eight piastres. I also gave a few piastres to my mother and grandmother Amalia, and they each bought me a few things like slippers, sherbet, a can of Brilliantine, and so on.

On warm nights we would sleep outside the tent, on the baker's plank, and I would cover myself with a sheet – white as snow, naturally, for Grandmother Amalia used to change the sheets twice a week – and towards dawn I would sometimes wrap myself in a blanket against the sharp, slight chill. To this day I still do not know of anything sweeter or more pleasant than sleeping like this in the dry desert, with its absolute silence and pure atmosphere, and the companionship of the workmen sleeping a short distance away, wrapped in their rags and woollen blankets, stretched out directly on the sand or on wooden tables.

I was a little surprised to see two of them sleep in a single blanket, wrapped tightly around them both. In the middle of the night I sometimes saw them, as if in a dream, tossing and turning, and from the single, amorphous mass of flesh would come a muffled groan and sighs of deep pain.

I would bathe once or twice a week when the lorry brought supplies of food and fresh barrels of water, which the workmen would unload carefully, as the water would spill over a little, splashing them and dripping off them.

I would let the cloth door of the tent down to the ground and secure it with pegs from the inside. A reddish light from the rays of the sun would spread over the cloth outside, with a cosy, glowing warmth.

As the fresh, invigorating water poured from the mug, making patterns in the tickly lather from the soap, I would enjoy my body, and my solitude, in a repeated erotic fantasy. A woman whom I knew as a partner, as a twin and as an equal – I would feel her curves and secret places, yet in the end she was a total stranger, foreign to me, her softness and roundness and her coquetry inflaming me and overcoming my inhibitions, but yet I did not know her, and however much I came to know her later perhaps I still do not know her. The woman of my dreams and love, my woman, the woman of my exile, cleaving to me, yet completely detached.

Sometimes I would spend hours wandering freely in the desert, closing the tent up after everyone had taken what they needed for the day, and wandering alone in the sand. I never let the tops of the telegraph poles disappear from my sight, however. These were my way marks to safety, and I was constantly checking that they were there (every moment, it seemed!), for I had read a lot about, and been scared by, the trials and tribulations of wandering in the desert. For all that, I was unable to resist the magic of the solitude and silence in the depths of the sand, when the tent and the workmen had disappeared, with the ballast machine and the smell of molten pitch, the black heaps of soft-bodied asphalt and gravel, and the tiny pieces of crushed white stones. I was sunk in my daydreams and fantasies, returning to the company of 'Umar ibn Abu Rabi'a and Majnun, and Buthayna's Jamil and Imru' al-Qays, to their lovers and sweethearts, and their fat-bellied Bedouin women with wide red cloths tied round their soft round bodies, their noses pierced with jagged-edged gold rings, and chins tattooed with two parallel lines, and dark blue colouring on their full lower lips, promising pleasure that was both carnal and refined.

I found a broad, highish hill, covered with pebbles of different colours, shapes and sizes, soft to the touch. There were conical ones, evenly-shaped ones, wavy, granulated ones, round and polished ones, long and thick ones, and thin, eroded ones – delicate white lines like hairs bunched around a grey circle inclining to black, and sharp, thin edges – the shining brown giving the smooth edge a softness at odds with its biting sharpness, while the shining white was dotted with fine spots that seemed to sparkle under the transparent pebble. Small sunken lines split the disintegrating carved faces. I said, 'The sea was here a thousand thousand years ago, the sea is still here, and will remain for a thousand thousand years.' I gathered together what I could of these treasures, lost with time. Had not every treasure been lost? Including the treasure of love? Were they not lost? Quick, sweet, soft bursts of laughter, one after the other, from a neat and beautiful mouth; brief glances, honeyed but sharp-edged, one after the other, from eyes completely calm; a boundless freedom within the soul; blue-winged birds flapping their wings expansively – had they been lost?

Every light has its shadow, of course, isn't that so?

Pure she was, pure she is, dark and cunning also, sometimes full of desire, but more often shy and reticent, like a child with her trusting nature and undisguised duplicity; sophisticated, worldly wise in her body, her boldness and her knowledge were frightening. She was

forward and petulant, meek, submissive, humble and obedient, but
fickle when I doubted her and my soul and my fate were in her hand
– was this her secret? Was she lost? Where had she gone?

On the mound of pebbles I stumbled like an intruder on the
head of a gazelle, a skeleton completely bare of any flesh, of the
stains of life, just a clean, strong set of white bones, the eyes two
hollow sockets opening through to the inner darkness of the skull,
nothing in it except the upper jaw with teeth still intact. The lower
jaw, which I never found, had fallen off. Where had the body
gone, and the rest of the skeleton? I kept the head, guarding it and
treasuring it among my meagre possessions until I was imprisoned
in 1948. When I was released, I only discovered that it had been
lost several years later. Was it really a gazelle's head? Uncle Farah
had turned it over in his dark, long-fingered hands, and said: 'A
gazelle, my boy! A little gazelle! Not yet weaned, poor thing!'

A short distance from the road I also came across a torn piece
of silk, decorated with fine lace. The desert and the harshness of
the open country had made the purple colour dry out and it had
become a very pale and dull red that had faded in wavy lines. It
was just a half-buried scrap in the sand, in a vast, moist depression,
a levelled cradle to which my erotic dreams flew, carrying my body
with them in their roamings. *Let me dream, passing stranger, for*
an hour in the desert. I do not know you, I will never know you, just
a dream that appears, with your cruel, loving eyes. Let me close my
eyes, then, over the two warm hills of your breast and forget restraint,
a body laden with ghosts, drunk on dreams. Do not look at me, please,
because in these eyes of yours I see caverns in which the darkness of my
soul flares. A furnace of dark fire. A harsh, radiant brightness that
transfixes. I cannot, no, I do not wish to see what is in your eyes. The
gleam of the sun's reflection and the roar of the whirlpools of hell. Do
not look at me, please. Do not know me, for I know you, my mistress,
my dream. My tears have dried up, it's over. Your inner fragrance
across the passions of the sand, the raging of my lust like the smell of
white honey with its waxen comb that has lost its life-giving nectar.
The henna flower between your thighs is tender, quick to moisten with
the dew, with soft hairs like wormwood flowers, yellow. Like flakes of
fluffy, carded cotton, though their fragrance has a heat and a fire
of amazing sweetness, a mad, muddled circle of confusion, coming
and going under the gaze of piercing eyes with their oppressive frame.

103

Your body is a jewel half buried in the sand, your breasts are firm and compact as they press down on me, crafty houri of the Nile, or a slippery, golden fish that slithers impatiently through my passionate fingers and leaps into the waters of the desert, cleaving its way through its depths that rise and fall in the light after the arid sunset, the woman of my imagination fleeing from me constantly though she lies in my bosom; no, do not whisper to me, your voice is confused and muddled, it will not unfold itself to me.

Sharp, warm, soft, studded with spikes like a prickly pear, she flutters within me like a bird of sacrifice, trembling with distant affection and with something that I do not understand and do not know. A hissing under the foot of an oppressive mountain, the smell of burning.

Be quiet, then, please, I do not want to hear you or even to know who you are – why all this beauty, all this remoteness? – the cruelty of absence is a powerful charm, attracting the soul of the infatuated man happy to be destroyed of his own free will. The sphere of the universe, your luxuriant hair, your strong eyes, the divinity of your voice has no equal, you say with all your emotion and passion, desire and distress, how can I say that you are not alone, so why am I alone, why, the more devoted to you I become, the more dumb I find myself, and whenever I burst into song, I start to stammer, why am I a prisoner? no, no, no, I mean that, why then do I just say I have yearned, I have tried to see, to hear, to know, to awake from the pressure of anxiety, I have grown weary of wandering and roaming in more than one tiresome valley, I am in a depression of sand and pebbles.

All right, my brother, then what?

The rustle of your silver jewellery on your silky neck never leaves me, never tempts me to twist it around, the hardness of solid diamonds on your fingers does not attract my hand. I grope for them, touched by God, driven mad by the torments of desire. Leave me, do not deprive me even of dreams, have I been fated to be deprived even of a dream? Your breasts throbbing under me are the wings of a tender broken idol past its time. I am tired of all that, nothing of it makes sense for me, the wreckage of clouds, exhausted incense, the rocks of passion, ruined and destroyed. 'How can the soul be at rest after He has called it?*' I have no liking for anything, boredom transforms everything, everything into silence, silence that in turn gives rise to a new boredom, the cycle has no beginning and no end, of course, what is after nothing? nothing, and time goes on, why does it too not come to an end, why? why? for no hand can wipe away this misery, no, sir, misery be damned, damned to hell!*

I loved him, and am finished.

Since it is I that have accepted he deserted me.

Not even in a dream.

My uncle Nathan would keep an eye on the workmen and supervise what they were doing. He directed them and spurred them on, sometimes barking at them, sometimes speaking to them quietly with his instructions. So the work would progress.

The British engineer stayed in the Rest House and came every day, at no fixed time, in a Jeep from the direction of the desert. He would get out, check, inspect and examine; sometimes he would be angry and fly into a rage, then quieten down and say: 'Excellent! Bravo, Nathan!' in his broken Arabic, pronouncing the name of my uncle the English way, with the second 'a' swallowed.

Farah al-'Arabawi chose a smooth, flat stone, which he cleaned with his hands, telling me to keep this stone for him in my tent, by the life of the Prophet! He set up a stove of solid stone, leaving an opening in the middle, in which he lit some pieces of wood from dry desert shrubs and old pages of *al-Ahram* with a match that he struck on the sole of his foot. He carried on tending the fire, feeding it with dry desert grass that he had gathered in clumps and which crackled in the fire, giving off a pungent, stinging, aromatic smell and white smoke, until the surface of the rock was hot. He told me to bring him (by the life of the Prophet!) a mug of water from the barrel in the shade behind the tent. I stood up and left him for a moment, and when I returned he took two handfuls of flour that he had done up in a soft parcel inside his sack. I knew from its smell and colour that it was flour made from a mixture of durra, fenugreek and barley. He mixed the flour with a little water. He didn't knead it, but flattened it gently and expertly on the warm, flat stone, patting it with skilful fingers to spread it out thinly, until it emerged, perfectly baked, as a round loaf with a penetrating smell. The lower part of the loaf turned red and I heard it throb as it flew off the surface of the stone, with a light steam wafting under and around it. Farah al-'Arabawi soaked some dry dates with a couple of handfuls of water and pressed his invitation upon me. I ate a thin slice of bread and two dates. The food tasted strange, challenging the tongue and the teeth with both pleasure and surprise. Uncle Farah's face lit up in a toothless grin, overflowing with a generosity and goodness that were almost childlike.

At the end of the day, when I checked the food store, I discovered that we were missing a packet of Abu Ghazala tobacco. I went back to count the packets, check the money and recheck the calculations. I knew where the packet had gone and I covered the cost from my wages at the end of the Friday. When Uncle Farah came some days later he said to me, 'It was me who took the box of tobacco, my boy. I know, I was reckoning that you'd do what you had to. What's a piastre missing for a few days, what's a box of tobacco?'

It wasn't the theft that hurt me and broke my heart so much as the betrayal that I saw in it. I said to myself that if he'd asked me for it I wouldn't have refused, so why didn't he trust me? Why didn't *he* do what he had to? It's not the theft, it's the deceit. Was it naivety and simple-mindedness on my part, do you suppose?

Why do they lie to me, I said. Why do they deceive me? Why, I said, come on, why should I be deceived? Why should *I* believe *them*? And forget? Something had broken.

No, sir, I said. All this for a packet of tobacco?

Obviously not.

Was it all of them, then, all of them?

Why did they lie to me, deceive me and tell me stories after that? To protect my feelings, fearing for me? Or out of pity and kindness? Or was it just disdain and disregard towards me? And why should I be deceived?

I didn't need any of this. Or anybody. How pressing was my need for this thing that I called truth. That I called love. And in my imagination there was no difference between the two.

My soul was nauseated by this destructive lying; it stank of ruin and desolation.

The murder of thousands, of tens of thousands of children through famine and the ravages of disease in the midst of ruins brought down by rocket strikes from the nightmare intruder, the lies of tyranny, the eloquence of defeat using shameful masks from a pile of clapped out, medieval inspiration, impotent lies sheltering behind worn-out slogans, the lies of the venerable chief of staff, may God protect him, the lies of the shaykh and amir, may God preserve him, lies that light fires, pollute the oceans and rivers, painting earth and heavens black, the lies of rulers and writers, of newspapers, radio and television, lies of enemies and friends alike, lies of love, lies of indifference, lies of the bed, lies from rostrums everywhere, from their Excellencies, Highnesses, Majesties, Graces, elite and riffraff, kings and beggars alike, alike, the lies of songs, the lies of books, the lies of false art, the lies of poetry, the most deceitful of poetry, the most lying, the most ugly, the most stupid, a continuous violation of all our homelands in the spirit, on land and beyond! I want to be set free, to be set free, to run as fast as my feet will carry me in the burning desert of truth, cleansed of every stain. Far from all lies, soaring free on my wings, in the vast expanse of the sky, calling out with all the strength of my joy in freedom: 'Aaaaaaaaah ... Aaaah!' There is nothing left for me but to confront the demons and to stare into their eyes without being turned into stone, I have not come to say 'Peace!' but to curse the entrails, smash the skeletons and rout the beasts of oppression.

I continued to wait for Farah al-'Arabawi to appear. The only thing, almost, that stung my heart when we left that place was that I never saw – and never will see – Farah al-'Arabawi again after that. I can still see him and hear his rough Bedouin dialect, though; some of his words I could hardly understand, as his hoarse voice emerged from the depths of his strong but emaciated chest.

We went back to Tarrana at the beginning of September, arriving at night. The barking of the dogs answered the howling of a wolf on the edges of the town. I was so terrified that my heart almost stopped beating.

The noise of the wild beasts of the night crowded all together in my breast, clashing together and spurring each other on. The echo of the weasel miaowing, her face like that of a monkey whose laughter echoes the clink of the jewellery he had stolen from Aunt Rosa and Aunt Salome's cupboard with the ringing sound of little bells, the squeak of the crawl of the salamander with the chest of a cooing pigeon and the head of a crowing cock dragging its long scaly tail with a dry clanking sound, the tops of the thick nocturnal trees whose luxuriant branches I hear chanting in a language whose sounds I do not comprehend, though my heart understands, while the hissing of the winged dragon mingles with the neighing of a horse with the head of a thundering lion, a gazelle's body and the hooves of a bull whose roar alternates with a deep-bottomed lowing, the gentle cry of the gazelle who swims with the body of a fish whose fins are the damp leathery wings of bats flapping noisily, whose regular beat I recognise in the overflowing canal, the snorting of the infidel jinn hidden in the jungle of alfalfa and henna behind the mill, whose edge throbs with his unique penis with which he rips open the vaginas of fallen women, the neighing of the penguin with horse's hooves standing with one foot raised on the edge of the threshing floor bathed in soft mud, the rumbling of the skink as it cuts through the midst of the night and the Nile, the gurgling of the water divided in two when ploughed by two parallel penises bursting from a belly which is the shell of a tortoise, the braying of a she-donkey sheltering in her pen, the flap of her wings beating uselessly, as futile as the wings of an ostrich, the flow of the milk of the ram with buffalo teats, erect one after the other, a great number of them, flowing with warm, white milk that gurgles in the earthenware pot that never fills through the night, the croaking of the frogs at the bottom of the water channels, with stork's beaks that peck at the flesh of the sheatfish gliding over the bed, the lowing of speckled wild cattle squatting in the water on the threshing floor, opening the jaws of an insatiable river horse, devouring enormous water melon seeds pregnant with the blood-red sweetness of ripe flesh, the rattle of the enormous snake as it crawls across the fields on a hundred small, pointed feet, scratching and ploughing the parched soil until morning to make it fertile, the whirr of the eagle's wings falling on the clover fields on the main canal with the mouth of a fish with countless teeth taking the durra grains into its mouth and pulling them off their cobs, sucking up the little fish from the water, the barking of an enormous fox lurking in the cotton fields striking the earth with its strong, sturdy trunk trampling with a camel's hooves on the blossoms the shitting of a goat with the jaws of a crocodile with a sharp drawn sword the sound of which I heard splitting the ancient Christ's thorn tree in front of the house.

Farah al-'Arabawi had said to me, 'Listen to your dreams, my boy, and follow their advice. Did you know that I listen to what is in my dreams, and follow in its footsteps?'

After my return to Tarrana, on 4 September 1939, I read an advertisement in *al-Ahram* following news of the declaration of the war that we know as the Second World War. At Samuel's, in the Carlton Restaurant and Bar on Alfi Bey Street (telephone 41800), there was lunch to order for 9 piastres and dinner *à la carte* for 12 piastres, with special prices for subscribers. When I knew Alfi Bey Street after the revolution I used to lunch in a Bulgarian or Armenian restaurant with Ahmad Shawkat, and pay (each for himself) seven and a half piastres for a hot meal with meat and dessert. Shawkat had taken his doctorate at the University of Tagore in India and joined the Foreign Service. Some years after that he worked in complex negotiations with Israel during Sadat's time, then served as our ambassador in Sudan. At the time I am speaking of, he lived in a furnished room in Falaki. When I met him once by chance some years later, I approached him with the same old enthusiastic affection, and a youthful naivety that long years had not blunted. He answered me with a cold, neutral '*Ahlan*! Hallo!' perhaps because I had called out to him 'Shawkat!' in great excitement, rather than addressing him as 'Ahmad Bey!', for example. I was with him in Alfi Street when I heard Gamal Abd al-Nasser announce the nationalisation of the Canal on Cairo radio in his unforgettable deep voice, 'in the name of the people'. We embraced each other on the street that night, made our peace, perhaps for the first time, with the 'Leader', and went to drink beer in the Carlton. Samuel had disappeared.

Packard, Ford, Chevrolet, Austin and Renault cars would sweep past me on the near side of the road (the original side), avoiding the other side of the road that had been widened and repaired, and whose surface was swimming in new pitch and asphalt spread on a layer of flattened, levelled pebbles and ballast. Sometimes I would wave at them in greeting, for no reason in particular, just to be friendly. Only a year later I was waving again with my hand, this time at open British army lorries with waterproof tarpaulin hoods stretched over their iron poles, covering hordes of young English soldiers going to dice with death in a way that usually ended in defeat. I would run with the lorry, or behind it, for a little, on the earthen Nile embankment in front of Tarrana, waving with my arms and shouting 'Down with the Nazis, down with Hitler!' The boy soldiers would look at me with slight amazement, indifference or fright. This boy with his galabiya and wooden sandals who ran along, pointing and shouting things that they usually couldn't hear because of the loud roar and steady clank of the engine. They were no doubt wondering about me a little apprehensively. When the war had ended, angry and agitated in Ramleh station, I would gesture at the same people in their open Jeeps with Tommy guns at the ready, 'Evacuation! Down with imperialism!' The British weren't as keen on exotic entertainments as the Americans were, but that didn't stop them staging the most extraordinary event to rival even the more unusual American novelties, for they had recently started – that same year, in fact – a swimming competition in the Hyde Park Serpentine, the first condition of the competition being that no one was allowed to enter it unless he was fully dressed, with a high top hat or a round bowler, a full buttoned waistcoat, heavy English shoes and a woollen suit. Would the Language Academy dare to try to revise the names of names of towns and villages like Nidbaba Tadrus, Kom Zamran, Minyat al-Khayt, Kafr al-'Itta, Kanisat Shabrato and Sayyid al-Iqliti, or even eradicate them altogether? 'I hope it never dares,' I said, as the flocks of fatted English lambs walked in formation behind their shepherd through the wide green meadows, content, happy and self-sufficient. Herds of Italian prisoners walked endlessly down the levelled road in the Western desert, their gamble finished, they had surrendered their hands to the emptiness of the boundless sand, the famous prisoner leaves his trench to fall on the Yankee's shoes, kissing them as the tanks and armour crush thousands, burying them alive in their trenches and underground fortresses, prisoners, refugees, dead men in their millions, or in units, a single individual always altering any figures, however astronomical they may be, in the Khmer Rouge's Cambodia, in Ogaden, in the mountains of Kurdistan and the foothills of Kashmir, in Mexico and Chile, in the foothills of El Salvador, in Katanga, in Zile, Harare and Musawwa, in Rhodesia, in the Belgian Congo, in Bosnia and Herzegovina, in Croatia, in Nagorno Karabakh, in Soweto, in Jerusalem, in the forests of Angola, the prisons of Mao Mao, al-Ansar (1), al-Ansar (2), and al-Ansar to infinity in the Negev, Tyre and Sidon, in Newcastle and New York, in the land of war and shelling and destruction of the spirit whose history never ends, dripping for ever with blood shed in vain.

The French sailor in De Gaulle's fleet, with a striped vest, blue jacket, and a beret with a round, red tassel on his head, gave

the Greek girl a defiant, uninhibited kiss on the lips at the little
Sporting station as he boarded the tram to go back to his ship
moored at Ras al-Tin, or by us in Dakhila which was still small
and desolate; Louisa, Mu'allim Shenuda the grocer's daughter,
whose body was in full bloom and whose bosom was like a Christ's
thorn, bent down and looked at me with a furtive but knowing
look as she piled up corn cobs in the murky shop, her firm breasts
only just shaking as she leaned over. The boy Barsum told me
that her body was hot and that she could do wonders. Oh boy!
The red hornets hovered and buzzed and swooped, with their
heavy, striped, cylindrical bellies and their wicked humming that
sent a shudder through my body. *My poor brother, Abu Amin, may
God inspire you with patience! My mother came from Damanhur,
sick with grief and extremely distressed, to inform me of the death
of the dearest thing we had, Ghannan. It was terrible, depressing
news, which hit me like a thunderbolt and completely shook me up. I
developed continuous diarrhoea until I became completely paralysed
and I have only just come to myself again. I have written you this
with tearful eyes and a trembling hand, asking God to inspire you
and his mother and ourselves with patience in our sorrow. Nathan,
8 August 1943.* I was holding him on my shoulders with my arms
as I brought him back from the doctor's surgery to the house in
Ibn Zahr Street, carrying him over the Ragheb Pasha tram lines
and avoiding the horse carts and the few cars in the noon heat. He
clung to my neck, desperately seeking support, as if he knew that
from now on there was no help for him. He had lost weight and
parts of his hair had fallen out, leaving bald, bare patches on his
head, which had now been painted with iodine and a cream with a
penetrating smell. The typhoid never left him; he would yell out,
screaming in a way that knew no reason, the sort of screams that
come from a body that knows it is dying but refuses to die. I could
do nothing for him, not I, nor anyone, and even now I do not
know how he died or where he has been buried. Was it pain that
made me forget? I know, though, that my father, his father, was
broken afterwards, and that he never stood up straight again until
he joined him, before a year had gone by.

The woody esparto stalks that grew behind the mill, though,
drank their fill of the victim's blood, turning into lewd women
who danced together in the gusts of the dusty *khamasin* with a

cry that could not be resisted. Their bodies were fresh and soft, two rows of tree trunks, wide-eyed deceitful houris with dark skins and gleaming complexions, with shoots of green herbage bursting forth from under their armpits and between their thighs, tender sprigs with sharp edges branching from their arms and legs, their kisses, and the bottom of the grave, a mixture of steeped poison and sharp-tipped honey, as they flit in the last light of the moon.

In the moon's bright light, pouring out mercilessly in the August night on the surface of Wadi Natrun, the plants have a metallic sheen, tombs stiff with white ice frozen over them, their breath heavy and warm.

Wasn't Uncle Nathan with us? I only know that he came at dawn after I had gone to sleep in the wedding tent, in the Valley. Was it the bridegroom's tent?

I know that we continued to cover great distances on hard footpaths between soft, tumbling sand dunes, under the grinding pressure of the moon, until my feet grew tired. Uncle Farah in front of us with his long, bouncing steps, walking in the desert like a person walking in his house, so that we could hardly keep up with him; but we hadn't yet arrived, and all sorts of tales and gossip were being passed around the little group. The foreman, a relative of the bridegroom, had invited just five or six of his colleagues, among them being Hegazi 'Awadin, Khadra's husband, and 'Awad's brother. The cold had begun to creep up on me. Uncle Farah took his shawl off of his shoulders and wrapped it around my back. It had the sweet smell of Abu Ghazala tobacco on it, and the fragrance of desert herbs. In the middle of the sand I spotted what looked like rubble – a few fragments of old stones, and signs with Arabic and French written on them. By the light of the moon I could read the names of long-vanished monasteries, planted in the sand between the ruins, and in smaller letters I could just distinguish: 'Department of Egyptian Antiquities'. 'Oh,' I said, 'how many monasteries, once full of faith and piety, are now haunted by the ghosts of seventy thousand monks! How many hundreds of cells and hermitages, caves and retreats!' Did I hear the echo of the monotonous rhythm of hymns – chants in the Coptic of the Pharaohs, a language abandoned but not extinct? Was it the scent of incense and candles that assailed me or was it the fragrance of the desert grass in the moonlight?

My legs were sinking into the soft sand, exhausted by the long walk. How long had we been walking? Three hours? I heard Uncle Farah say in his hoarse voice, 'Hukriyya is to the right now!'

I saw nothing, understood nothing, and did not bother to ask. Walls of pitch black shadows assailed me in the bright moonlight.

We felt the ground slope down beneath us, as the sand became harder and more solid under our feet. Uncle Farah pointed us to a patch gleaming with silvery salt in the grip of the moon. I remembered Bobello and felt a longing for Sitt Amalia and for the warm, narrow bedroom in the house at Tarrana.

I ate the piece of lamb and rice with my fist dripping with fat. I was hungry, almost dead with hunger, as I watched the dancer dancing in her gold-spangled, transparent costume, with her wide red sash wrapped around her full hips, turning under the circle of her bare brown belly, emphasising its mystery and its invitingness and accentuating the smoothness of the conical mound beneath it. She had plump and obviously tender limbs, that shook to the rhythm of a crude and primitive drum, the thump of blood pulsing in a new, youthful manhood, stiff from the meal of lamb's meat and lust for half-forbidden female flesh, with the whisper of the castanets on her fingers, her jewellery rustling in time with the yellow spangles on her dancing costume, with the rattle of the gold necklace with the seven strands ('Hollow, no doubt!' I said to myself, 'or else she would not have been able to bear its weight on her golden throat'), the coarse, snakelike bracelets and the thick, open anklets with the two square heads. The pipe and drum, with the smoke from the honey flavoured tobacco and the hashish, filled my blood with the blows of early despair and youthful lust at the height of this night of ecstasy.

Suddenly I felt my uncle Nathan bending over me and waking me. 'How could I have left you to sleep here on this mat?' he said, as if to himself.

I had been sound asleep. As a place to lie down, it seemed to me more comfortable even than my bed at home.

The rug was rough and stained, as I now saw in the light of the lamp that had begun to get dimmer and brighter again with a spasmodic hissing. Uncle Farah's shawl was covering the striped woollen blanket they had placed over a dry, solid cushion when the sudden onset of sleep had made me lie down suddenly.

I saw Uncle Farah asleep, too, on the sand in the courtyard that had now begun to empty as the noise of the wedding died away – a courtyard roofed with old, dry palm leaves and beams made from the wood of sycamores, through which I could see the few remaining dawn stars shining in a sky whose pure, radiant blueness was infinitely transparent.

8
Sarah and Wadida

Uncle Fanus married Aunt Wadida, in spite of the fact that he was dying of love for Aunt Sarah, her younger sister.

I will never forget the look of love in his eyes until the end, despite his marriage to her sister.

His faithfulness to her was absolute. Although he had had three sons and four girls by Wadida, he continued to look at Sarah with the same look of love until the day he died.

His white, fine-boned face, a little square and thin, possessed great strength. Though his sight was weak and he had a slight squint as a result of an old infection, his deep black eyes always had a gentle twinkle in them – that is how I knew him. His soft, combed hair was always carefully cut, and he wore a clean, ironed skullcap, or on special occasions, a fez. His peasant galabiya, of expensive wool in winter and white poplin in summer, never had a stain on it, winter or summer.

I overheard Grandmother Amalia saying, in words whispered to Aunt Rosa and Aunt Salome that I was not intended to hear, that Uncle Fanus had broached the subject of his wish to marry Aunt Sarah with Grandfather Sawiris. My grandfather already knew about it, and so did we. And that Grandfather Sawiris, without anger, indeed, with an understanding, almost, of the torment in Uncle Fanus' heart, had told him what we had all been expecting, and what my uncle Fanus had been the first to realise. Sarah was the younger sister, as we all knew. Did he really think that the elder sister should remain a spinster? 'But, of course,' said my grandfather, 'Sarah's sister is yours for the asking,' Was there anyone more deserving of her than her cousin? Who better to take care of her?

My uncle Fanus agreed without a moment's hesitation. Had he

in the depths of his heart prepared himself for this outcome? Was he in the depths of his heart fearful that his love might fade, as love usually does?

Was he really wanting to conquer this love himself, so that it might remain for ever?

It remained alive. Love.

Have I killed my soul's passion and lived without a soul? Or is it that by killing the soul, it lives?

Oh, Uncle Fanus! How could you sacrifice the whole of your life in order to gain it?

How could you bury the sufferings of an unbearable love? Where did the lacerations go, that ripped apart your soul, leaving it in tatters? Always with the blood hidden, in secret? In secret?

Shed unceasingly within, unseen by a single eye? Were they spent in vain, without meaning, these sufferings and lacerations?

As if it was necessary for suffering to have a meaning, any meaning!

Oh, my grief, my love!

Is there no end to this wailing and lament for misfortune?

Where have these unendurable sufferings gone, the sufferings of a child, the sufferings of a youth, the sufferings of a grown man?

Valueless.

Suffering has no reward.

My eye lighted on a dark-skinned maiden as the dew fell, and her hair by night on her fair cheeks fell. I asked her to come with me, but she said, 'Young man, go back, don't die of love,' and the dew came down.

For several nights, preparations were made for the wedding that I did not attend. I only found out about it from Uncle Nathan's letter to my father. He wrote that the wedding had been celebrated with the Lord's blessing in Tarrana church the previous Saturday evening, that the people of Tarrana had joined the wedding procession, more Muslims than Christians, and that Dawood's family had even opened the big house specially and had sent their son Anis, who was studying medicine at the Qasr el->Eini college in Cairo, to congratulate the couple and invoke blessings on them.

At the end of the following year we found out that Anis had shot himself for love of a dancer he had brought back from Cairo and whom his elderly father had taken for himself. The shot echoed around the sleeping farmstead from the house where Anis Effendi was staying, after his father had turned him out. He had resorted to a sort of doss-house intended for seasonal workers. Hearing the shot, the villagers, tossing and turning in their heavy sleep, thought that one of the guards was firing his rifle to scare someone off, or else out of boredom.

Rahma would sing peasant wedding songs to Aunt Wadida in a thin, muffled voice that sometimes failed her, *May he make your years with your husband tranquil*, and Khadra would tap the drum after warming its taut skin by the fire of the 'Sheikh Ali' lamp, beating it in a lively but unvarying rhythm in the guestroom courtyard spread with mats and rugs, while we rested on hard cushions stuffed with cotton in front of the wide door under the long, flowing branches of the Christ's thorn (or was it a sycamore?) tree, that hung down from the empty area in front of Grandfather Sawiris's house.

Linda would look at me as she squatted on the mattress, with those slightly protruding, slightly bulging eyes of hers.

Ah!

For the first time now, in the evening of my life, I realise that these eyes have been pursuing me across time, they are just the same, unchanging, the same look in them with multiple meanings, layer upon layer, looks of understanding and enquiry, strangeness and temptation, a little contempt perhaps, a little gratitude perhaps, incitement also, and disdain, provocation undoubtedly, and a desperate plea for help as well. And also love? What is the meaning of love? Sometimes two honey-coloured, very Coptic eyes, with the colour and sweetness of honey and Nile flood water, sometimes two yellow and greenish eyes, and sometimes two deep, pure black wells. But always large and wide, always deadly; I die of love for them, they are always the same, these eyes.

Linda snatches the veil from Khadra ...whose soft, rich, massaged hair is uncovered. She laughs shyly, her femininity laid bare. Linda puts a sash around her waist and dances alone, a lithe, supple body, responsive and arousing, in a dress that I suddenly notice clings to her belly, her backside and her breasts. She is all virginal and exciting in her long, dark yellow outfit scattered with extra delicate red flowers, pleated, but a little too wide, almost revealing the ankles and bare feet I had seen her rubbing with pumice stone, then putting in a bowl of clean warm water with a little olibanum dissolved in it to soften her skin, so that it would become tender and pink, and any trace of roughness would completely disappear. These feet skipped up and down, light as two birds, on the spotless, gleaming yellow mat, stepping over the surface of my heart and teasing my new found masculinity, aroused and throbbing, that I strove to conceal in the folds of my white galabiya, fearful of wetting it and disgracing myself.

Even Hamida the leper, who had retreated into a corner in the shadows, hid her face with the edge of her veil as she swayed with the songs. *She was white and wearing a white outfit. It is not easy for me to leave you, but I can't get your father's approval*, you whose breasts rise with the sweetness of white doves, bursting from your bosom and flapping their wings continuously in fields thick with esparto, scrub and prickly pear, oozing with salt, *Pretty bride, talk gently, musk and amber we have burned for you*, arms of incense, delicate and transparent, embraced your naked belly, the tentacles of an octopus almost waving, almost visible, almost tangible. From your shoulders fell the veil and shawl, with their writhing serpents and their fringes that hiss and glisten, *Oh mother of locks, Oh white one, and the girls clap on the quiet mastaba to the beat of the drum, Oh you of the locks, her breasts are pomegranates of Paradise, her hair hangs down like thickets, and her rump is like a water-melon from the Nile islands, Oh the Sweets' Merchant*, the muffled shrieks of mocking laughter from the girls as Khadra bursts into loud laughter, with her soft, full, sweet voice that slips from between her red thighs that are suddenly smashed with the sound of a dry rumble, and collapse in tiny pieces whose taste in my mouth is strong and sweet. *May he make your years with the bridegroom tranquil!*

The breast's nipple is a protruding wooden teat, spouting from the rough vein of the Christ's thorn, and the cheek is a polished metal plate. The vagina is a broken cup, with an open cavity, and her belly is hollow, carved from a sycamore tree streaked with plaits of fine, wavy hair, embedded in the flesh of the wood. The humming of bees, the roar of the engines of the Packard truck, the rumble of the heavy lorry cutting its way through the flood water and the heart and with a foul, monotonous, mechanical noise, the threads of passion are neither cut nor forbidden. *May he make your years with the bridegroom tranquil!*

As for the bridegroom, he bowed his head and smiled, listening to the songs and the drum with one eye on the dancing and the other on a game of cards with my grandfather Sawiris. Gorgi the precentor was following the game with his ears. 'What did you throw, Fanus, my brother? What came up for you, Ba Sawiris? Be careful, my brother!' Suddenly, there was a barking of dogs under the massive Christ's thorn tree that cast its boughs over us and made the open space in front of our house frightening and dark.

I filled the pitcher with cow's milk for him, not wanting either the pitcher or the cow's milk, wanting only you, light of the moon ... wanting only you, light of the lantern ...

Fanus, Fanus, your severed head turns in the circle of the sun that appears from the water of the Nile as Salome dances for you in her seven veils, your broken body filled with the Holy Spirit in the church of the Virgin at the head of the square of the barefoot, the square of the naked, the square of the downtrodden, as Father Andrawus blesses it, sprinkling water from the great marble baptismal font whose weight has made the church foundations subside a little beneath it, and whose ancient wood has split.

These are women's wiles, they gird themselves with snakes and wrap scorpions around their heads.

How I miss the scalding heat of the sun and the fruit of the artichoke.

I put you in my hair, my brother, and plait it around you.

I put you in my eye, my child, and put kohl over you.

And between my breasts, my brother, and swaddle you.

How I miss the beating of the snake in the heart of the lotus flower.

And between my thighs, young man, and put a sash over you.

And if your mother comes to me looking for you

I will swear faithfully that he never came to us.

Khadra's voice, intoxicated with wine before she has even drunk. What will she be like when she downs the cup full of intoxication? She stood up now and left the drum to Rahma. Its rhythm immediately changed to a gentle trickle of tunes, one after the other. She swayed and strode, she danced and played, she came to me shaking her belly before my eyes with a movement that came close to revealing everything, without quite giving way to temptation. The little group stared at her, delighted to witness her dancing skills at first hand. Fanus gazed at her as if bewitched. 'Is this beautiful?' she asked directly. 'Yes,' they said, 'yes, mistress, unequalled in beauty, everything you do is beautiful.' Then she said, 'But what I'm going to do now will be even better, my masters!' She threw her arms apart, and suddenly she had two broad wings with thick, silky feathers and long, soft fringes. She flew off before our eyes and went to the top of the old Christ's thorn tree. Then she said, 'When the wretched lover comes, worn out by the long days of separation, and yearning for union and embrace, when he is battered by the storms of desire, let him come to me to the islands of Waq Waq.' I carried on plunging into the seas and journeying through the horizons, but I had no port, a dance, but no reunion.

The woman's dance, in a dream, means her fall into disgrace, this was the interpretation of dreams. My woman's dance has not been finished for many seasons. The dance of my imprisoned heart, though, is proof of release from the chains of love. Will it always know how to dance, or will it stay shackled and fettered for ever and ever? Isis, Khadra, Rahma, Rama, Linda, Loris, Ni'ma, for which of you is my love destined? My seven houris, soaring with outspread wings in the vast regions of the heaven of my soul that is ever without fixed horizon. You, the single, repeated one, did you find the lost part among fourteen drowned in the region of Kemi's body, did you breathe life into the bones of a corpse? When you return to me, you return unceasingly, unceasingly, gasping for breath from the dance of desire and eternally unfulfilled lust, the dance of destruction to wild music, loads weighing thousands of tons, explosions of devastating impact, the screams of 170,000 children dead from cholera and famine, the gurgling of water in streams polluted in the name of liberation, the dance of lies is so easy and effective, the earth subsides under its buildings, the silence of the ruins returns, O ruins of Rama, effaced but never forgotten in the soul of the passionate lover, battered by love's catastrophes without end; the weight of tranquillity is unbearable.

My shirt's worn out, mother, my breasts show through it.
Market tomorrow, light of my eyes, I'll bring you a better one!

The fangs of hidden pain still bite, I am still unable to groan, or to stifle my groans, my bones are sagging and the scraps of old cloth have been folded away.

Oh, your hair is a camel driver's ropes, and I sell my soul ...
Oh, your thighs are marble columns, and I sell my soul ...
Oh, your belly is leavened dough and your breasts are perfect pomegranates ...
And the navel is the bottom of the cup ... and the navel ... the bottom of the cup, the navel ... the navel ...

The boats cast off, ploughing through the canal, their sails tied back like folded wings, trembling under the storm, the river Nile overflowing with incense of ambergris, hoes loosening the ground and turning it. Is it Jesus with head turned down on the arm of his mother, having fallen from the cross with no resurrection? With a pained look on her face she examined me sadly, and in a soft, loving voice, as if she wanted to hide that love from herself, as if she was ashamed of herself, she said, 'I only wish I knew what it is that pains you, my beloved, what it is that keeps you away from me and from everything.'

Matisse's dancers in the courtyard of the naked, among them that frightful monster with a beak like a claw and eyes like fish eyes, his penis a sharpened tooth with a pointed tip, and her body offered up in front of the beam of light from an open window with curtains so flimsy they might also be light. She said, 'It is like making love in the middle of the road.' Her body is soft as silk, light of light, I see the strong tree trunks spring up from the ground like columns flying in the seas of passion towards the heaven, their luxuriant green branches shading love's suffering and the torment of its ecstasies. Her hands hide her fair head and her face cowers under the veil that hangs over her wavy hair, dangling like the night that has only just passed. The dawn awakening burns with a never-ending fire.

Aunt Wadida, the expected bride, was taking part in the singing with due caution and reserve, not wanting to be betrayed by her happiness. Her happiness, however, overflowed and flooded her face, despite herself, and her eyes sparkled. Meanwhile, Aunt Sarah had mixed the drinks of sherbet and presented them to the bride and bridegroom (both of them loved and both of them traitors), and to the male and female guests, passing them around on the *mastaba* in tall, thin cups of fine glass, with tapered waists and gilded edges, by the yellow light of the Sheikh Ali lamp, whose shadows quivered on the walls.

121

Father Andrawus had come on Saturday afternoon with Mu'allim Gorgi and the lad Barsum, who had put on a bright-red deacon's sash over his sparkling white galabiya. They spread incense through the whole house and the Mu'allim chanted hymns of praise and blessings, accompanied by Barsum.

Father Andrawus opened the big government ledger and wrote in it a record of the betrothal and registered the names. Uncle Arsanius, the father of the bridegroom, was in the house with Uncle Selwanes, his two daughters Linda and Rahma, and their cousin As'ad Effendi. Uncle Nathan was there too, and my great uncle Yunan, who came from Alexandria at midday and stopped the taxi he was driving for a living in the open space in front of the house under the sycamore tree.

We stood on the open *mastaba* behind Father Andrawus, who began, *In the name of our Lord Jesus Christ, the Redeemer, we are here to celebrate the betrothal of the blessed Wadida, daughter of Sawiris and Amalia, to her fiancé, the blessed Fanus, son of Arsanius and Victoria. Let us pray and say together: "Our Father ..."*

When he raised his head and right arm to say the Lord's Prayer, so quiet, quick and garbled that hardly anyone could hear it, the sleeve of his wide black cloak fell from his arm, and a large, green, veined tattoo of the cross could be seen on his right wrist. We were following him and responding to him, *Oh true Lord, the Word of the One Eternal God, Oh you who gave human kind in betrothal to eternal joy,* when he quickly, almost mechanically, mumbled, *in His sublime and glorious incarnation. His slightly nasal voice became louder, We beseech you, only-begotten Son of the Father alone,* crying, *Oh God, pour forth of the clouds of your pleasure the rains your favour and blessing; make easy for us what we have gathered to perform in this place, and command for this undertaking of ours a good beginning and a praiseworthy end.* His voice dropped as he quickly walked back and forth, mumbling something unintelligible, until suddenly he resumed his chanting, to be a pure and lawful betrothal and a prelude to a glorious marriage protected by God, that the bride and bridegroom may be softened with the burnishments of pleasure and enjoyment, grant them sound and mutual love. The wave of prayer subsided for a second and there was an indistinct stirring, until the wave rose again in a climax, Grant them perfect happiness, and give them pleasure at the time of joy at the festival of crowning, Amen,

Our Father who ... and he sprinkled the blessed water with the drops of oil from the sacred chrism on the head of Aunt Wadida, on the head of Uncle Fanus, on the door of the house and on the ancient marble threshold engraved with hollow, sunken figures and writing in hieroglyphics now worn away by the march of footsteps over them, and the rubbing of the wide wooden door.

Was it then that I heard my Uncle Fanus calling anxiously in a muffled voice, 'Bobello, Bobello, your name is my salvation, for I am throwing myself into the depths of the ocean accompanied by prayers and supplications in Coptic and Arabic'? Was it now that he threw himself from his brown-skinned rock with its gentle, mellow surface, in which alone was his salvation and his landing-place? It was no longer possible to go up to it again now, ever. He fell, while the chants of benediction rose up around him.

The next morning, one of Hemeida al-Zi'rani's children came to me, a peasant from the Abu Dawood estate and a sort of odd-job man in Uncle Fanus's office. With him was the lively white donkey ridden by my uncle Fanus to get to and from the estate.

He kept the accounts, administered the estate and supervised the farming activities.

I met the boy out of breath, saying that Khawaga Fanus wanted me now.

Between Tarrana and the farm one could reckon half an hour's riding on a strong and lively mount.

I used to take every opportunity to ride this splendid donkey, racing along on it whenever I could. It had a high back and broad chest, and was well bred, with a quick intelligence. As soon as I climbed onto its back, it would neigh like a horse, only more hoarsely and with a rougher tone. I would sometimes give it a handful of fresh, green clover at sunset, after Uncle Fanus, our next-door neighbour, had come back home, and it recognised me.

I set out on the back of the donkey without any hesitation, kicking its sides hard without respite, clasping the reins firmly but lightly as the noble beast galloped me along the Nile embankment, raising its head proudly as the wind whistled in my ears. The lad Khalaf had been covered in dust as he ran tirelessly some distance behind me, smiling provocatively whenever I looked at him, confident of catching us up.

My uncle Fanus greeted me with hands stained with henna. A very faint reddish-brown colour spread thinly over the palm and fingers between the areas that had been left white, as the hand and fingers were bent while being dyed. I had not seen the bridegroom being tinted in henna.

'Never mind, Uncle's boy!' he said, though of course, I wasn't really his 'Uncle's' boy, he was the son of my grandfather Sawiris's brother. His father was in fact my grandfather's cousin, and I used to call him 'Uncle' out of politeness. 'I was wanting you to do a couple of sums for me and "white" them out neatly.' (he lisped a little when pronouncing his r's), 'I've got to finish the boss's ledger now, Da'ud Bey is in a hurry for it.'

The task occupied me for about two hours in a building made of mud bricks that the peasants called 'the office'. The wind blew onto it straight from the Nile. The fresh air alone was reward enough for the task and the boredom of the calculations but I also collected a large, shining, silver five-piastre piece, which for a while I had pretended to refuse, although my eye was on it. He said to me, 'Write it down in the accounts, my boy, and don't worry! Five piastres won't hurt Da'ud Bey.'

I had lunch with him. We cooked a dozen eggs over a fire of dry corn cobs, with some sour cheese, and purslane fresh from the fields which we washed in river water from a clay jar. Its taste on my tongue was pungent, coarse and raw, but we followed it with a guava sweet as honey. 'Never mind, lad,' he said to me. 'You know the expression "the lover's onion"? You know that as well as anyone!'

After lunch we relaxed outside, in the shade of the 'office' wall, on a mat of durra stalks. Uncle Fanus asked me, a little shyly, about my aunt Sarah. I told him, with great pleasure, how Aunt Sarah had gone with me to the Coptic Orthodox al-Karma nursery on my first day there. It was a foul, muddy, rainy day, but Mansur Effendi, the nursery supervisor, received me like royalty. Was I five? Perhaps. From the very first glance I fell in love, as I usually do, this time with Miss Catherine, Miss Catherine with the waxen face and angelic look. I discovered that I had to repeat after her, 'cat, mat, ran, man' to pictures of a cat, a mat, a boy running, and a man putting on a hat. I also told him how I used to wake early, with the morning star, in the house in Number 12 Street in front of the mill and the girls' school. I would creep into the quiet, sleeping house (full of warm breath, nonetheless), go to Aunt Sarah's and Aunt Wadida's room, lie down between them in their bed in the early morning, and fall asleep.

He listened to me with his whole heart as if he had forgotten the engagement and his heart's sacrifice.

I was shy of telling him, however, that about that time I also used to watch in fascination a ritual for preparing a special waxing paste to make a woman's limbs shine, how the paste was made with lemon and sugar, put in a pan on a paraffin stove with a low flame, and tossed until it turned into a soft, spongy, rubbery dough.

The paste now set, with a firm, even texture, and was spread out on the clean, shining tiles in the narrow passage between the two beds in front of the open window, while I lay under one of the beds. When the paste had cooled, my aunts pulled off some pieces and began to work them, moistening them slightly with a small, fine trickle of saliva from a tightly pursed mouth, then spreading them out with quick, successive strokes on their outstretched legs, bare to the top of their thighs, and then quickly pull the strips off all at once with a 'flop, flop' sound. The red and black colour of the tightly woven cloth at the top of their legs could be seen indistinctly, shining in the light from the window, but would then vanish with the movement of spreading, grasping, and slow stretching of the paste, and the quick, sudden pulling off of the paste, whose floury colour had by now become a little dirty. The two women would laugh from the sting as the wax was torn off from the strong, solid flesh which turned red and glowed, tender and very soft. I remember the fleshy sound that alternated-- one moment the noise of paste sticking to their legs, the next the violent parting from them – as the two women groaned.

A henna paste from Baghdad had been applied the evening before to my aunt Wadida's hands and feet, then pulled off with roughly that same sound and the same rhythm. Linda, Rahma and Khadra shared in the henna, and the happiness, and after they had finished with it, Hamida the leper spread the henna over her hands and feet herself, alone, without anyone else helping her.

As I was going in to sleep, at the end of the evening, I heard my grandfather Sawiris in the other room say, 'My love, our Lord has forgiven Mu'allim Gorgi, he's hidden himself away in Heneina's house since the day he married, him and his brother Basili, dear, oh dear!, ever since the wall of the church fell on Basili, he hasn't spoken a word, he's been silent, he can't even drag his feet or move his hands.'

'He has to be carried and put down like a baby, dear, oh dear! And she's hidden away at home as well, no-one hears a sound from her.'

'Oh, she's hidden herself away, has she?' said Sitt Amalia. 'You know the saying: "When water turns to milk, the whore will repent". We'll see tomorrow!'

Grandfather Sawiris replied, 'Umm Yunan, fear God where women are concerned. You've got daughters too!'

'Jesus, forgive me,' said my grandmother.

Despite that, I was annoyed with Grandmother Amalia and my heart was heavy. I loved Sitt Heneina.

I went into the room I used to sleep in, with my sisters and Aunt Sarah.

It was the first room after the *mastaba*, with my grandfather and grandmother's room next to it. Opposite it, across the courtyard, was the animal pen, with just Mabruka, the buffalo, and Nu'ayma, the goose, the ducks and ducklings that waddled as far as the canal by day and came back at dusk (they had neither name nor leader) and the chickens. I loved the smell and fertile atmosphere of the pen.

We all used to sleep on a high, wide bed made of unbaked bricks. Underneath it was the opening from the oven, blocked up now during the summer, but which was lit during the winter to heat the room. I climbed up into my usual place between Aunt Sarah and my sleeping sisters, on the thick, soft mattress of cotton pressed straight from the field. You could just see the wick of the 'Sheikh Ali' lamp through the window specially carved out in the wall below the picture of the Virgin that was surrounded by a light layer of soot from the gentle flame that burned in a lamp made from a tin can. Its wick was sooty by now, burning on the surface of a little paraffin, with a slight but penetrating smell in the heavy, torpid atmosphere of the room, an atmosphere that as the night went on, was fragrant with the slightly sweeter smells of stored fenugreek and the contents of the other storage baskets – small, dry loaves of pitta bread with layers of durra bread on top of them, large circles of crispbreads, beans, lentils, durra, clay jars full of old cheese, whey with hot peppers, preserved and covered with clay and dry rags, pots of vinegar and black honey, butter with a little salt sprinkled on top of it. The black pots with round bellies, lined up on the floor, made me think of the ghosts of the night, and their varied smells, and the ghosts whose appearance they took on, were penetrating but not threatening. At the end of the room was a clothes chest in which I put my own few clothes beside those of my aunts Sarah and Wadida, and my sisters Aida and Hana – my other galabiya, two or three changes of underclothes, the suit that I wore to school and travelled in, an English woollen jacket, and some short brown trousers, protected with mothballs.

Anxiety, plus the excitement of the singing and dancing, the prayer service, and the henna, meant that I had some difficulty getting to sleep, despite the fact that I was extremely tired. I felt Aunt Sarah beside me breathing with difficulty in the murky darkness of the night. She was not asleep and I was also extremely angry with her. My heart was with her in the anguish that she had skilfully and bravely disguised, hidden even, throughout the day and night, but had now come back to haunt her. But I was also happy for Aunt Wadida, who had gone away to sleep with my grandmother and grandfather in the other big room with its enormous, tall grain silo, firmly shut, with just a small hole in it that was opened to bring out enough for grinding each time, and was then shut up again immediately with solid, moistened clay, after the grain had trickled out.

After the heavy air-raids in which the *Piazza* and Bab Sedra in Alexandria were destroyed – places which I now missed intensely – my uncle's wife Esther came with her children and took this room. My grandfather, grandmother, Aunt Wadida and Aunt Sarah went to sleep on the mastaba in the open air for some nights.

Uncle Yunan used to come every Saturday to spend two nights with his wife and children and leave on Monday morning after breakfast.

Before breakfast on Sunday, early in the morning, Aunt Esther would open the door that had stayed closed behind them all night, and would throw a bowl full of water and soap onto the ground in the courtyard, in front of the door of the room, making a little pool that quickly dried up. At breakfast, her round face radiated beauty, contentment and happiness. Her bright blue satin nightshirt exposed the tops of her arms and was deep cut, revealing her ample bosom. Over it she wore a thin, dark-red, filigreed shawl, in order to appear decent in the morning in the company of my grandfather Sawiris. But the folds in her night shirt left lines in the shiny material that could not be disguised – lines that wound under her full, round belly.

At night, through the mud wall, from the room next door I would hear sounds that assailed me as I lay half awake, half dreaming, muffled sounds like groans or whinnying. My night and my dreams were filled with the story of the beautiful woman bewitched by the ghoul and turned into a milch cow, who moaned at night and demanded that her husband break the spell and destroy the ghoul's handiwork.

I would gaze at the ceiling of the room, gloomy and distant, as the shadows and darkness came and went across it.

The wooden beams that supported it were pitch black on both sides of the room where they came down to rest on the edge of the two walls, the outer wall of the entire house, that adjoined Father Arsani's house, and the other wall that overlooked the courtyard, with a single narrow window in it with one closed wooden shutter, locked from the inside with a small, round, rusty iron bolt that was difficult to move.

The window was slightly open now, the night was warm, and through the window I could see a chink of the night sky with its many stars, cut through by the leaves of the tall, single palm tree that my grandfather Sawiris claimed to have planted himself as a young man, fifty years ago, or possibly more, perhaps ten years after the Urabi rebellion.

Aunt Sarah whispered to me, 'Are you still awake, my love?' I felt her arm stretch out to me to embrace me, and between her arms I found a haven from anxiety, as she rocked me in my flustered state and reassured me. My galabiya was raised up over my legs as I drifted off into the first stages of sleep, and the softness of her legs brought back to me the softness and tranquillity of the world. I saw Louisa, the grocer Mu'allim Shenuda's daughter, giving me a tin of Abu Ghazala tobacco for Grandfather Sawiris. I had been wandering around in the night looking for the shop but not finding it, while the fear of getting completely lost was making my heart race and taking away my breath. Then suddenly I found her, with a teasing look in her eyes, the look of a peasant girl who has just acquired a womanly shape and who knew it! Her breasts were still very small, but stood out firmly, like a pair of cones under her striped, coloured dress of fine material. Did she wear anything underneath it? Her legs were slim, delicately tucked under her dress as she climbed onto the low wooden chair with the three thick legs that Uncle Suryal had made. She stretched out her arm to bring me the box of tobacco from an upper shelf. Her laugh was hoarse as she threw her head back with girlish flirtatiousness. The red braid handkerchief at the back of her head slipped down, and her brown kinky hair appeared, with the two plaits gathered together in a loosely piled bun. I knew, or at least I imagined, that when she let them down they would reach to the top of her thighs that were now tightly closed and which, by their very meagreness of flesh, were arousing.

Tarrana, 22 November 1943.

My dear brother Abu Amin,

I present to you, to Sitt Sausan, to the Ustadh and to the dear girls my greetings and my many wishes, wishing for you all a continuation of health and prosperity. I was in Damanhur from Wednesday, left it on Saturday and met my wife Wadida at Itay al-Barud station. We came to the village together, with God's protection and Jesus's blessing, where our daughter Sa'diyya informed us of your welcome for her and your kindness towards her as soon as she had arrived at your house, that she had spent the whole of her period of residence in Alexandria with you, and that she was very happy. I put my trust in your munificence, for you are fully worthy of that trust, and you will find me grateful for your many favours and for your sincere love and fine feelings. It is small wonder that when the Ustadh, your son, was with us in Tarrana at Daud's estate he behaved in exemplary fashion – like father, like son, as the saying goes. We ask our Lord, may he be praised and glorified, not to deprive us of your love. From here, Wadida, Sa'diyya our daughter, Umm Yunan, Miss Sarah, and above all Uncle Sawiris and all the family are well, and send you our sincerest greetings. We hope to hear how you are, about whether the raids are continuing or not, and about

the health of the Ustadh and his success in studying engineering under
your auspices, and that is for our peace of mind.
    Your sincere brother,
    Fanus Arsanius.

Just a month before the death of my father in December of that
year.

Two years (or three?) after I had left Tarrana at the end of the
summer.

They took the bull out at the height of morning from Aunt Rosa
and Aunt Salome's pen, having put a garland of yellow sunflowers
around its thick neck. Hegazi, Khadra's short, stocky husband,
pulled hard on the rope. Under the enormous Christ's thorn tree,
it found Shaykh Alwan's cow, tethered to a stout wooden stake,
fastened with thick nails driven in to the tree roots. The cow was
restless, lowing and moaning, wanting to be mated but almost
fearful of it at the same time. The village children had gathered
in a wide circle, but now the men shooed them off. 'Out of the
way, child, you, and him, out of the way, son of Hannuma! Watch
out, my friend, the boy's a bit thick!' Suddenly the bull lunged up,
unsuccessfully, and fell back. It turned around, its nose running with
a stream of white fluid. Bellowing fiercely, it charged and turned,
but the twisted rope in the hands of Hegazi and his brother 'Awadin
(who had planted their feet on the ground, with all the strength and
force they could muster) kept the bull inside the unbroken circle.
The bull was striking its horns on the ground, then raising them.
Then it again raised its forelegs and this time mated with the cow.
For a moment, as the coupling reached its climax, it froze – the
actual penetration almost invisible. An anxious silence descended
on the gathering of men and children – and on the women, who
had hidden their faces behind the doors of their houses, giggling
with suppressed laughter. Then a cheer went up again, a great shout
of thanks to God, and excited yells of 'Hey, hey, God is most great.
Yes, sir, a real bull, that!

I slept restlessly. The smell of warm, rich buffalo dung, an almost
human smell, wafted in through the half open window.

The wise, knowing monkey was standing erect on the top of the
lofty hill of Bobello. He seemed almost to be there with me on the
ground. I could see him very close, his corpulence, his knowing smile

and his turquoise necklaces, staring at me with stern, understanding eyes, I knew them, a halo of light revolved around his head, his hair was combed and smoothed with Brilliantine, looking in a broken mirror, I could almost stretch out my hand to him. Entreating and complaining? Or grateful and sympathetic? The ring of faint rays formed a circle, sparkling, gleaming as it revolved around the thick hair.

The potsherds of thick, green glass were embedded in the wall of the big house that seemed either to burst from the heart of Bobello or to seek refuge inside it. The house's many trees seemed to have merged with the ruins, threatening them and driving them out. Behind the church a crack would suddenly open through which I could see a spacious courtyard stretching into the distance between the piles of rubble and the dust of centuries. I was afraid to step into it, but I could not stop myself going in. The monkey stretched out its clenched jaws towards me. I could feel the puff of its warm breath on my face, very close, closer and closer ...

I jumped up all at once.

My awakening came as a sharp jolt, violent, loud and sudden. My whole body was thrown forward as a result of it. Neither Aunt Sarah nor my sisters felt it.

I got down off the bed slowly and carefully. I went out into the deep blue glow of the night sky, whose surface was pricked by endless needles of light.

The courtyard was silent. The warmth of the buffalo and the hens squatting in the closed pen spread itself over me as I walked across to the clay jar resting on its slightly twisted, round iron pedestal. Under it was a small, clean basin into which dripped pure water, drop by drop, *tak tak tak*, almost soundlessly and very slowly, across the apricot stones that I could see at the bottom of the jar under the clear, gently undulating water. I dipped my mug in it and drank greedily, feeling that my thirst was unquenchable, even unknowable.

9

A Dry Fruit

It was nearly twelve o'clock, nearly noon.

The long express train went past, rattling over the sleepers in the distance. It gave a long whistle. The wheels clattering over the rails echoed rhythmically on the horizon over the fields.

'Please, sir, could you possibly...?,' Mu'allim Gorgi said to me, 'could you possibly pass by our house?' He wanted me to bring him the amber prayer beads that he had forgotten under the cushion. Sitt Heneina would know where they were.

Sitt Heneina's house, where her new husband Gorgi was now living with her and Basili, his paralysed brother, was set on its own at the end of the village, with the high Nile embankment on one side of it, and on the other Sitt Heneina's field, onto which the door of the house opened directly.

The old, deserted waterwheel was situated a few paces in front of the house.

Everyone knew, of course, that it was haunted and that 'they' – we were careful in what we said about them – came out for passers-by either at midnight or at the height of noon. Someone going past with not a care in the world would suddenly find his donkey in front of him – the donkey that he had left grazing in front of his house or in his courtyard. He would find it standing there, silent and submissive, with no bridle or packsaddle, as if it had lost its way or had simply wandered into this spot, precisely in front of the waterwheel.

More fool him, though, if he tried to get on his donkey, the familiar donkey that he knew so well. If he did, the donkey would suddenly rear up with him, rear up higher and higher with almost lightning speed, as its legs grew longer and longer and its head rose level with the tops of the palm trees, all the while braying like a laughing hyena, then toss him, the rider, off and throw him to the bottom of the waterwheel, from where he would be unable to get up again. The only escape for him, or any other unlucky person, from the wicked jinn's back, was to plant a knife in the name of Father and of the Son *and of the Holy Spirit, One God, Amen, in the name of God, the Merciful, the Compassionate, and through the power of the 'Throne Verse' or the Sura of Ya Sin*, between the wicked jinn-donkey's flanks, while he recited either 'Our Father, Who ...' or else the *Fatiha*. Otherwise, he would be found by some passer-by, or rather, his corpse would be found, beneath the waterwheel – and we all knew what that meant, even though the incident would be recorded in the government file as being an act of fate. The *'umda* would account for it to the police assistant or public prosecutor as a fall during the night from the high Nile embankment onto the hard wood of the waterwheel, whose water had dried up a long time ago – maybe, that is, most likely – only God really knows.

Uncle Gorgi knew that I was a rash young man (have I stayed so rash until today?). He knew that I had no compunction about provoking the jinn, and other spirits, at the height of noon, and that I was not afraid to pass by the old waterwheel or venture on to the stone causeway that jutted out into the Nile where the river sprite, or water houri, would appear with her thick black hair tumbling down over her naked back, her pert breasts gleaming white from behind the strands of her thick silky hair. She would entice men, snatching them off into the depths where she would add them to her endless husbands collected over time, whose corpses would never ever be found. Or else the corpse would appear by the bridge at Itay al-Barud, or on the shore of one of the islands in the Nile, bloated and mutilated, eaten by fish. Then we would know that he had failed with her and that she had thrown him out.

The previous day, we had been sitting under the great Christ's thorn tree, a large circle of men, Grandfather Sawiris, Father Arsani, Uncle Nathan and Uncle Yunan together, Uncle Fanus and his younger brother Barsum, and myself. Hegazi, Khadra's husband, was also with us, and Uncle Milad who looked after Grandfather Sawiris's farm.

Uncle Yunan seemed sleepy and lacking energy. He had come from Alexandria late on Friday evening. Just before dawn, we heard the splashing of soap and water on the ground in the courtyard, and my aunt Esther, whom I loved, disappeared and did not emerge from her room until the end of the morning. Uncle Yunan attended the engagement ceremony, signed the register and blessed the happy couple almost incidentally. The following day, he would travel back to Alexandria after noon, to earn a living for himself and his children in the enormous old taxi that shone with its nose high in the air, as it were, as if it had just come out of the factory.

We were sitting, in no particular order, either on mattresses placed on low chairs, the work of Uncle Suryal, or on a hard cushion thrown on top of a broad tree trunk that had been cut down ages ago, firm on the ground, its surface black and shiny from the generations of families in Tarrana that had sat on it, or on big, white rocks, or on a smooth-edged piece of marble with traces of engraved but faded drawings. Could it have come from Bobello? Or else we sat directly on the ground; is there anything better than the goodness of the earth? That's where we come from, every last one of us, dust to dust …

Uncle Yunan sat up very straight, a picture of pride and distinction. My aunt Esther would go out to say goodbye to him, bidding him farewell with her small, moist, compact hand, as she lowered her head and gave him a private, surreptitious look after yesterday night. Was it a look of possession and anticipation, of gratitude and contentment, of warning and expectation all together? Grandmother Amalia would take him to her dried-out bosom, whose love was as wide as the earth, and pray for him as she prayed for me. It is true that the dearest child is the child of one's own child. But her prayer for him had the warmth of a deeper passion, perhaps, for he had left now for the territory of another woman. 'May he preserve you for your youth, your children and your wife, my beloved', she murmured. 'My heart, my breast and my bosom are happy for you, son of my womb, Yunan, I am pure and proud; may Jesus accept my prayers, as many as the hairs of my head and the hair of my body. I pray, Yunan, son of Amalia, that you will prosper and succeed and may Christ preserve you in your comings and your goings and keep your every step safe.' She made the sign of the cross on his head quickly, lightly and almost secretly, as if she was ashamed of her love for her firstborn son.

134

From on top of the fire, Milad lifted an enormous pitcher, black with soot, which whistled as it boiled. The fire was dancing in the air, raising its tongues of flame aloft, as it quivered and flickered on the improvised stove that he had made in the open space beside the trunk of the ancient Christ's thorn tree.

He poured the tea, dark, strong, and pitch black, into small cups of fine glass with slender waists on a wide brass tray which Khadra had brought from Aunt Rosa and Aunt Salome's house. The thick liquid went down into the cups, foaming slightly with a rich swishing sound. Its taste was bitter, pungent, aromatic and extremely sour, with a fragrance that made one bite one's tongue. I drank it at one gulp, the only way to bear the burning taste.

Uncle Fanus suddenly lifted his shaved head in its clean, ironed skullcap, as Aunt Sarah passed quickly and gracefully in front of us, with steps at once bold and embarrassed, in the direction of Father Arsanius's house. In his eyes he had that look of love that instantly recognises and acknowledges the deprivation imposed on it (without accepting it), and submits to its fate but without being happy with it.

From the house came sounds of shouting and muffled laughter from the girls, among whom were my sisters Aida and little Hana.

Uncle Selwanes the tax collector was telling us a story about a service-taxi driver in Shebin al-Kom – the sort that travel between the villages and hamlets – who killed his little sister in order to get her jewellery. He said that the neighbours heard her shouting and imploring him to stop, they saw her falling on the ground to kiss his feet, but he pulled her inside the house by her hair and shoulders. They thought that it was some sort of affair of honour, and that he was avenging some family disgrace, so no one intervened. He smashed her head with a hammer, sold her jewels, travelled to Alexandria and spent the money on his girl-friend, a dancing girl. He said that the police knew her name – Su'ad Fahmi – and that she worked with the Beba troupe at the Monte Carlo Casino on the seafront.

Silence and sadness overcame me. When I had seen a picture of the dancer in the *Monday and the World* magazine it had aroused my erotic fantasies, and I felt as if she had betrayed me.

When the third glass of tea came round, sweet as honey and light as sherbet, I suddenly realised that I had not even been conscious of the second one that I'd taken from uncle Milad's hand. A 'medium' round of tea, middling in everything, both in its sweetness and in its strength.

Father Arsani was looking at the circle of men sternly but lovingly, his skin so delicate that it was almost transparent. But his bones were solid. The green, veined mark of the cross on the side of his forehead was almost invisible now, after how many years? His ironed, white galabiya radiated cleanliness, serenity and beauty. He lifted it a little off the dust on the ground. His thin feet were encased in leather slippers. His white round skullcap (of the same material as his galabiya, naturally) had been pushed back a bit and he looked very happy and contented at that moment, did Father Arsani). Why, do you suppose? His rough, wavy hair was elegant, grey but still vigorous, short and clipped, and gave one a sense of enduring youth. 'Tell me, Sawiris,' he said suddenly, between sips of the tasty tea. 'Don't you visit Wahba any more?'

I sensed that Grandfather Sawiris was surprised by the question.

'Come on, Arsani,' he said: 'I was with him in Cairo a few months ago.'

'And how is he now?'

'OK. The same as ever. How would you expect him to be?'

I knew, though not in much detail, that Father Wahba, Sawiris's brother, had been in the 'yellow palace' of the mad-house in 'Abbasiyya for years.

It was a place that inspired awe and dread in my heart.

I imagined it as a lofty fortress painted dark yellow, firmly locked, with towering pillars and blocks of rooms, and spacious halls where people walked full of dignity and self-importance, neither speaking nor answering questions. There would also have been locked cells with iron grilles, holding people fettered in irons, groping around and shouting out with no one to answer them.

The story of Father Wahba was a taboo subject, for no one could tell me what had happened to him, and to this day – when everyone else has left this earth (some returning to Bobello, some buried in the graveyards of Chatby or El Minya or Mar Gorgis in Old Cairo) – I have never succeeded in discovering what the story of Father Wahba was exactly, or why he was dumped in 'Abbasiyya. Was it because of a dispute over a piece of land, the distribution of an inheritance, or an old tale of love and murder that one could not talk about? Had there been a lover, whose body, bearing the marks of passion, abused and hallowed at the same time, had been hidden by night without any funeral rites, and then lowered into a grave in Bobello with no name or cross on it?

My mother said to me once some years later that she had visited him in the 'palace'.

She said he had been calm and content, with a radiant face, as if he were still a young man of twenty, or timeless and ageless. She said he had recognised her and called her by her childhood name. 'Labiba, how you've grown!' he had called out to her. 'Have you married and had children, daughter of Sawiris? May our Lord spare them for you.' 'How is your father Arsani? And your mother Amalia?' She said he was like a saint.

'Why are you crying now?' he had asked. 'You seem to be upset … there is nothing precious in this life, Labiba. Tell them in the village that I don't want visits. They are all with me, night and day. Go home now, my child, may God bless you!'

Her eyes glistened with tears as she told the story.

Father Wahba died forgotten, aged almost eighty, or even more, but he was buried in Bobello, as was right.

Uncle Fanus saw to all that.

After we had drunk the third round of tea, Father Arsani turned, his eyes still sharp and piercing as a hawk's, and called my sister Aida whom he was particularly fond of, and for whom he kept a special place at his gatherings and in his heart. Was it because she had a young, extremely dark face, and wavy hair? 'Come here, my girl, my precious girl,' he said to her. She was shy in front of all these men but not overawed by them.

'Read us a bit from *The Thousand and One Nights*,' he said. 'Where is the book, Fanus?'

His son stood up obediently and brought the book from inside the house.

'Where did we stop yesterday, my girl?', he said.

Aida read to us in a voice that was soft and gentle but very clear and confident. Because I knew *The Thousand and One Nights* almost by heart, I knew that, without any shyness or hesitation, she had just passed over those passages that call a spade a spade and had carried on reading – as if that was simply the right thing to do, as if she had not been aware of anything obscene or excessive in them.

To this day, after a full half a century, yes, I still miss her slight lisp and special tone of voice. My heart trembles when I think how I have lost her – sister, companion, my other half almost, irreplaceable by anyone else.

Aunt Sarah came back with Linda and Rahma, the three of them making their way in front of the men to return to Grandfather Sawiris's house. Their heads were lowered as they looked at us with eyes full of innocent wiles. Uncle Fanus's face turned red. He had always been quick to blush and he would continue to be so until the end, especially when he had had a bit to drink. A florid red blotch would appear on his cheek bones under the fine, taut skin of his face, and would spread almost to his hooked, supercilious nose.

The smell of rich food, sweet and satisfying, wafted over to us with the smoke from the big oven in the courtyard of our house. Sitt Amalia was cooking two male ducks for dinner.

Saturday night, then.

Uncle Yunan arrived, in need of reviving. There was a smell of smoke from the burning stalks of dry *durra*, cotton firewood, palm leaves, and broken wood from the Christ's thorn tree that I had stripped some days ago with axe blows to the edges of the ancient tree's branches, while Sitt Amalia shouted to me from below, 'That's quite enough, my boy! Careful you don't go any higher!' I was intoxicated with the feeling of adventure, however, as my body teetered on the high, thin branches that shook, threatening to break off at any moment as the blows from my axe stripped away the thin edges that were good for fuel, while the smell of sap from the green flesh of the wood, and the air filled with greenness from the leaves of the tree rustling densely around me with a slight sweetness, made me all the more intoxicated by my death-defying struggle.

How drunk I became, I, even before tasting it. Your wine brought me to the ground. How did I find myself drowning in the violent throes of your body?

My drunkenness is a vessel swept away by the ocean depths.

I have no port.

To this day.
To this day.
Uncle Fanus wrote my father a slightly official letter of condolence, according to the rule book, after the death of 'Ghannan', my younger brother Emile, from typhoid after a long period of suffering. I never knew any brother apart from him. My sister Aida had died two months before him from the same disease, but Hana and I escaped.

I found the letter on paper yellowed with time, with pale blue squares on it.

Dear Abu Amin,

I offer you, your wife and the children my greetings and best wishes. Sitt Umm Yunan came to our house yesterday, with God's protection, though her health is precarious. We learned from her of the death of your child Emile and God knows, we were very upset. But I am confident that you are a man of wisdom who knows God, and whoever knows Christ will find peace. We ask mercy for the deceased and patience and consolation for yourselves. Wadida my wife shares in your grief and sends you her greetings. She is sorry that she cannot come owing to the fact that my mother has been in Damanhur for about a month. Sarah's eyes are bad, but she may come to see you soon. Here everyone is well and sends you their sincerest greetings.

Your brother Fanus Arsanius,
Tarrana, 17 August 1943.

Just four months before my father was to die.

I said, 'May God have mercy on you, Uncle Nathan. When you wrote your letter of condolence, at least you did not resort to cliches about patience and consolation and peace – or look for excuses. No, bereavement made you ill, and laid you low with grief. You were truly warm-hearted.'

I said: 'Have you come to call people to account after they have died, and had their fill of death?'

'Yes', I said.

I could not be bothered with any of that.

On 14 May 1948, I was sure I would be arrested that night.

I had read in *al-Ahram* that a stray child, a girl of seven months, had been found dumped in the Waili religious court building. The police had also found a two-year-old boy straying in the Waili administrative district, a five-year-old boy called Muhammad Hasanayn in the Old Cairo district, and a four-year-old boy called Sayyid Muhammadi in the Shubra district.

Stray children.

And that the prosecutor's department had appealed against the verdict issued by the Waili district court for the acquittal of 'Abd al-Rahim Ragheb, who had been charged with possessing a bomb, and had set the following day for determining the appeal.

I heard from Rahma that a middlewoman, originally from Damietta, who did the rounds in the area, had heard the news of my Uncle Fanus's engagement to Aunt Wadida and had come especially from Shibrin el-Kom with all sorts of Dumyati piecework with fast colours, veils, gauzes, Edko dresses, crepe veils and silk crochet-work for sale by the metre or by weight, as the client wanted. She also had all sorts of silks, frocks, dresses and cotton, and gaberdine from Damietta. Aunt Wadida had haggled with her until she almost ruined her, the middlewoman, born and bred in the market.

She bought from her cheaply everything needed for her trousseau.

His Majesty the King was sitting, in all his youthful, radiant, shining splendour, his young face bright and glowing, in the royal carriage that carried him to the parliament building on the day of its inauguration. The carriage was closed, with golden ornaments, and behind it stood two grooms in their special uniforms, standing upright on the platform that had been fitted behind the closed body of the round carriage. An emblem of a gold crown was fixed to their red tarbooshes.

The road was completely empty and deserted.

The noon day heat fell on me mercilessly.

I passed beside the old waterwheel, about to enter Sitt Heneina's house, to ask her for the amber prayer beads from under Uncle Gorgi's cushion.

The sant tree called me, its hair tumbling over its naked breast, yellow, almost white, with yellow flowers in it. Its body was tender as it swayed, softly and gently, inviting with an irresistible force. She was there before me, available, offering herself with open legs.

'Come, my darling, don't go to her, come to me, in my arms I will give you pure honey to drink. Come … c - o - m - e.'

140

Her plaintive cry flowed into my blood, numbing me.

I found myself unconsciously walking towards her, on the verge of falling into her embrace.

Suddenly, at the last moment, I stopped.

I found myself on the edge of the well by the waterwheel. Almost sucking me into it.

Slowly, I recovered my wits, released from the spell, and from the blaze of the noontide fire.

I rushed headlong towards Sitt Heneina's door. The door was shut. I knocked on it gently and it opened of its own accord. A gentle, merciful darkness enveloped me in the shade of the trees in the courtyard, sycamore, guava, palms, Christ's thorn and mango.

I crossed the end of the courtyard, shaded with a leafy bower of vines, comforting with their sweet, sugary smell, a very little overripe, a swirl of tender, imprisoned sap on the point of bursting out from under their juicy skins. The smell turned my head.

I found myself on the threshold of the one large room, where I fell into the grip of something even more enthralling. In a darkness of a special kind, a visible gloom like a very dim, deceptive but pervasive light, I saw her with my uncle Basili. I saw him crawling feebly, dragging his body along by pushing his hips and elbows against the dirty floor of the room.

I saw her lift him from the ground, his arms and legs hanging down lifeless, raising to her his wrinkled, cracked, imploring head, and it was as if some light of suffering was blazing from his eyes, in that luminous darkness. A stifled sound, something between a moan and a death rattle, escaped from his open mouth. Was this a sigh of tearless weeping?

Every part of the paralysed body was an open, gaping mouth, in which the lips turned, and a powerless tongue twisted in its cavern. Without a sound

Every part of the beaten body was an eye dying with a desire to speak, to say something, to shout, to bellow. Without a sound.

Hands clutching at nothing with twitching fingers, stretched out as far they would go, bones tense and taut, stabbing at the air and sinking into it with no resistance. But the hands were floppy, powerless to enforce their will, without a sound.

The remains of the body that had once been young and strong still preserved a mask of strength, but only on the outside. All strength had been drained from it. Only a heap of fallen stones remained there, the force of a will that no one could resist, but which there was no way – no way – to fulfil.

His will was that he should be free, be free. But he was dumb. Everything in him was dumb. How strong was his ringing, silent shout, overlaid by groans and an exhausted sighing, overlaid by silence.

Heneina lifted him from the ground and put him on the bed with his head on the long pillow.

From behind the lace curtain, lightly spotted with black, I saw her throw her veil aside and let down her black outer dress, her coloured undergarment, and her pistachio green satin vest from her bosom. Her neck escaped from the neckline, as she pulled her arms out of the sleeves with a rapid movement whose firmness and precision startled me. Her clothes were bundled up around her middle and rested on her huge hips.

Her enormous breasts were like spheres filling the universe, but their beauty and youthfulness took the breath away. They were firm, and their nipples were long and erect.

She gave him her breast to suck.

I saw only the eyes of a broken, noble wolf.

I was not aware of myself, it was as if I had been stolen away.

I tell myself now that I was not an intruder come upon an erotic scene. No, rather I was captivated, as usual, by a vision, a vision like a prophecy.

The emaciated lips first closed slowly and tentatively over the nipple, then the mouth closed over the firm, white, enormous breast that now settled over the thick moustache, over the beaten face, with its rough, unshaven skin and closed eyes.

Her breasts were dripping not with lust but with the milk of compassion, consolation for a loss that could not be recompensed.

Not out of pity or regret, but an affirmation of her womanhood and his thwarted manhood.

A victory for the woman, as mother and lover.

To make love was her doing, not his.

Hers and hers alone, for all the injured and all the fallen.

The sick and exhausted.

The failed and disfigured.

Was that a humiliation for all men, a revenge on all men, on her father whom no one had known, on her dead husband, and the blind man thrust into her bosom by the power of the angel's sharp sword?

The firmness of a woman's tender rock, filling every gap, and every gaping mouth.

A safe haven amidst the depths of the vicious, stormy waves.

Here, I can hear the secret calling you.

How much of my spirit have I spent on you, and have *you* gained anything?

As for me, I have gained through you something that I cannot do without.

I fall, with my love, into the darkness of grief.

Tuesday, 13 Tut 1708
24 September 1991

Notes

Chapter One
1. 'Monday and the World'.
2. 100-pound notes.
3. *Book of Songs*, a famous work by the classical Arabic writer Abu al-Faraj al-Isbahani (AD 897 – c.972).

Chapter Two
1. A suburb of Alexandria.

Chapter Three
1. Hot, desert wind.

Chapter Four
1. A famous dictionary by al-Jawhari (d. 1003).

Chapter Five
1. Twelfth month of the Coptic year.

Chapter Seven
1. From the Anglo-Egyptian Treaty of 1936.